Robert J. Conley

Barjack and the Unwelcome Ghost

LEISURE BOOKS   NEW YORK CITY

A LEISURE BOOK®

September 2009

Dorchester Publishing Co., Inc.
200 Madison Avenue
New York, NY 10016

ISBN 10: 0-8439-6225-9
ISBN 13: 978-0-8439-6225-3
E-ISBN: 978-1-4285-0733-3

Visit us online at www.dorchesterpub.com.

BARJACK AND THE UNWELCOME GHOST

Chapter One

If you've been keeping up with my tales, you know that ole Butcher Doyle come out to Asininity from New York City just only to kill my ass for that time I kicked him in his balls whenever we was just snot-nosed kids. And you also know that Butcher's old man was the head of the Five Points Gang in the city. Well, now, I don't want to waste too much time a-telling what I done told before, but I got to tell a certain amount just in case you somehow or other missed the last tale. The long and the short of it is this here. Butcher changed his damn mind about killing me, and I went and made him a depitty. I already had me one depitty what was pretty damn good, although I sure as hell don't want him hearing about me saying that. His name is Happy Bonapart. So they got me outta the trouble I was in, and then there I was without no problems and with two goddamn depitties on my hands. I reckon on account a' the boring and peaceful times, I shouldn't ought to a' been surprised none about what happened next.

Butcher come into my marshaling office—oh yeah. In case you didn't already know it, I was town marshal of the little ole town of Asininity, and I also owned the one and only saloon and whore-house what was allowed to run in that town. One a' the benefits a' being the local law. So Butcher come into my marshaling office while I was setting there behind my big ole desk, and he walked right up to the desk and plopped a sack on top of it. I looked up at him.

"What the hell's that?" I asked him.

He reached down and loosened the cord around it and then tipped it over, spilling out a whole bunch a' cash. My eyes musta opened up kinda wide, and I looked up at him again.

"One more time," I said. "What the hell is that?"

"Well, it's money, boss," Butcher said.

I heaved up a long sigh, and I said, "Well, hell, I reckon I can see that it's goddamn money, Butcher. What the hell I'm wanting to know is where the hell did it come from, goddamn it."

"Well, now," he said, "I just went around collecting it."

"Tell me from who you collected it and what for you collected it."

"I collected it from all the merchants in town," Butcher said, "and I collected it from them in exchange for keeping them safe."

"The old protection racket, huh?" I said.

"That's right, boss," he said.

"Goddamn it. Butcher, set your ass down."

He went and dragged a chair up right close to my desk, and I seen the really proud look of him, and I kinda hated to wipe that there look offa his face, but I knowed I had to do it.

"Let me explain some things to you, Butcher,"

I said, and I opened up my desk drawer and brung out my bottle a' favorite whiskey and a coupla' glasses and poured them full. I shoved one over to Butcher and he tuck it. I tuck my own self a drink. "We don't do that ole New York City protection racket out here. That's what the hell they pay us for, keeping the citizens safe from crooks and all. So we don't do it that other way. Now, I know you ain't been out here long, and I ain't explained ever'thing to you, but we just don't do that. So I reckon you're just going to have to go back around and give all this all back."

"Give it back?" Butcher said, sounding real god-damn astounded-like.

"That's what I said, Butcher. Give it all back."

"Now?"

"Right now."

Butcher stood up and went to scooping up the cash what he had spilt out and stuffing it back into the bag, and I can tell you what, his face was wearing a long-ass look on it.

"Something else, Butcher," I said.

"Yeah?"

"I wish you'd cut it out a-calling me 'boss.' It sounds too much like you're still a part of a gang in New York. It just don't sound right out here."

"Well, what do you want me to call you, then?" he asked me.

"Barjack is all right," I said, "or just marshal. Either one. It don't matter. Just don't call me 'boss' no more. Okay?"

"Yeah. Sure, Marshal. Whatever you say."

He'd done scooped up all the money, and he

picked up the sack. He turned and walked toward the door with his head a-hanging real low. I felt kindly sorry for the son of a bitch.

"Butcher," I said.

He looked back over his shoulder.

"There ain't that big a hurry," I said. "You ain't finished your whiskey yet."

He come back over and set down again and picked up his glass. He kindly smiled at me then, and he tuck another drink.

"I guess I still got me a lot to learn," he said. "It's like you said. I ain't been out here very long yet. Hell, back home all the cops takes payoffs."

"This here town has been real good to me, Butcher," I said. "I got my marshaling job, and I got the Hooch House, and I got the royalties off a' them damn silly books that ole Dingle writes about me. Hell, I don't need no more money. And if I ain't paying you enough, hell, if you need any money, just ask me. I'll take good care a' you."

"Okay, Marshal. I'll remember that." He finished off his whiskey, and then he stood up and picked up that money sack again. "I'll get this back to them people now."

"All right, Butcher," I said. "That's good."

He left the office that time, and I let him go. When he was gone, I just kindly shuck my head a little. I hadn't anticipated nothing like that, but a' course, I reckon I should've. Ole Butcher, he was all right. He just only didn't know nothing about nothing but his city ways. Then too, he just weren't very damn smart. It seemed as if I always had that problem with my goddamn depitties. They'd do any damn thing I asked them to do, and they was goddamn good men to have beside you when times got tough, but they just wasn't none too bright. I guessed I'd just have to learn to live with that.

Well, I drained my glass and got up. I figgered I had done spent enough time in the marshaling office for one day, so I headed down the street for the Hooch House. Along the way I seen that goddamned pettifogging Peester what was our town mayor and the one what had hired me in the first place to be town marshal. I nodded at him, and he kindly grumbled at me and went on by. He was a-headed toward his office. I went on into the Hooch House, and soon as ole Aubrey, our barkeep, seen me, he poured me a tumbler full a' my special good brown whiskey and tuck it over to my table where ole Bonnie Boodle, my partner in the Hooch House and my special woman, was already setting with my other depitty, ole Happy Bonapart. I set down with them and picked up my drink and had me a good gulp. Bonnie grabbed on tight to my right arm what was the closer one to her and snuggled up against me, wriggling her fat ass around in her chair.

"What's up, Barjack?" asked Happy.

"Not a goddamn thing," I said.

"I could do something about that," said Bonnie.

"Not now, sweet tits," I said. "Maybe in a little while."

"Is anything wrong, Barjack?" Bonnie said.

"Ever'thing's just fine," I said.

Just then a cowboy at the bar knocked the shit out of another puncher and sent him sprawling on the floor. He walked over to stand up above his victim and commenced to telling him to get up and have some more.

"Take care of that, Happy," I said.

"Yes, sir," Happy said. He stood up and pulled out his six-gun, walking toward the cowboy. When he got right up behind the bastard, he raised his gun arm up real high, and then he brung the barrel down as hard as ever he could right smack on top of the cowboy's head. That cowboy made a little "whuffing" sound and dropped straight down onto the floor like a sack a' flour. Then Happy collared a couple a' stiffs and told them to toss the lump of cowhand outside. He give a hand to the other puncher what had been knocked down and helped him up to his feet. That puncher stood up a-rubbing his jaw.

"You okay, ole pard?" Happy asked him.

"Yeah," the puncher said. "I will be."

"Aubrey," Happy said. "Give him a drink. Whatever he wants." He left that puncher at the bar and come back over to the table. I was thinking how ole Happy had handled that real well. Just like what I woulda done, but I said to him, "You're real goddamn free with my booze, ain't you, pard?"

"I'm sorry, Barjack," he said. "I just thought—"

"Aw, shut up," I said.

Ole Flossy Applewhite, what I had just recent allowed to deal cards in the place at a table in a front corner a' the room, raised up a glass toward me as if he was a-toasting me, and he smiled. I just grumbled. Just then I heared a voice from back behind me what sounded like as if it was right by the front door.

"Hey," it said. "Looky there. What's that?"

Then another voice said, "You can't come in here."

I twisted around to look, and I seen a Indian, by God, walking into the place. He was dressed mostly like a white man, but he was a damn Indian for sure. I figgered him to be somewheres between thirty-five and forty years old. He was wearing two six-guns, and he had on a black vest and a black flat-brimmed hat with a red-tailed hawk feather tied onto the hatband. I stood up right away and walked towards the door, and ole Happy, he was right close behind me. Two men at a table by the door had done stood up too, and I figgered it was their two voices what I had heared.

One a' the men was ole Oscar Martin what run the hardware store, and the other'n was his running buddy ole Harry Henshaw, the gunsmith. They was stepping around the table looking as menacing as they could manage.

"Did you hear me, Indian?" Martin said. "I said you can't come in here."

"Let's throw his ass out, Oscar," said Henshaw.

I stepped up just about then, and I said, "Now, just hold on, boys. If anyone gets throwed out a' the Hooch House, it gets did by me."

"Hell, Barjack," said Henshaw, "we just thought we'd save you the trouble is all."

I looked at the Indian. "Mister," I said, "is you really a Indian?"

"I'm part white," the Indian said, "but I can't prove it."

"Does the white part a' you have the price of a drink?"

"Yes, it does."

I turned toward Martin and Henshaw. "Boys," I said, "there's only two reasons how come I ever throws anyone outta the Hooch House. One is if he's causing trouble. The other'n is if he ain't got the price of a drink. This fella here don't qualify on either one a' them counts, so you two just set your ass back down and mind your goddamn manners."

Well, they looked at me kindly unbelieving and then give each other real questioning looks, but they set back down and didn't say nothing more. I was damn curious about our Indian visitor, on account a' we didn't have no Indians nowhere near around Asininity. I was standing right smack in his way a' walking on into the place. I looked him in the face, and I said, "Come on in, pard. If you'll join us over at my special table, I'll buy your first one."

He looked around a bit and didn't see no other friendly faces. "All right," he said, and he follered us back to our table and set down with us. I looked at him again, and I asked, "Whiskey?"

"I don't mind," he said.

I waved at ole Aubrey and helt up my empty tumbler. When I seen that he had saw me, I called out, "And one fresh one." Well, he brung a fresh one, and I pointed to the Indian. Aubrey set the glass on the table in front of him. Then he poured my tumbler full again and went on back behind the bar. The Indian picked up his glass to take a drink.

"Barjack," said Happy, "I ain't looking to cause no trouble, and personal, I don't really care, but ain't it against the law to serve alcohol to Injuns here?"

"I ain't never heared a' no such law in Asininity," I said, "and that's all I give a shit about."

"Yes, sir," said Happy, and then he looked over at the Indian. "No offense, sir."

"None taken," the Indian said.

"What name do you go by, pard?" I said.

"My name is Moses Red-Tailed Hawk," he said, "but that's a little awkward in English, so I just go by Mose Miller."

"I'm Barjack," I said. "I own this place and I'm the town marshal. This here is my depitty Happy Bonapart, and this is my sweet-assed Bonnie Boodle."

Ever'one howdied each other all around. But I weren't yet satisfied. "Where you come from, Mose?" I said. "Not from around here."

"No, Marshal," he said. "I'm up from Indian Territory. The Cherokee Nation to be exact."

"You a Churkee?" I asked him.

"Yes, sir, I am."

"Well, don't pay no attention to those shit-heads over yonder by the door," I said. "You're welcome in here any time. I sure as hell ain't got nothing against Indians, especially Churkees. If you don't mind me asking it, what brings you all the way up here?"

"I'm chasing a man," he said.

"What for?"

"To kill him."

Well, that done it. It went and got real quietlike around the table then. Final, I broke the silence.

"Has you found him here in Asininity?"

"I just got in, Marshal," he said. "I don't know if he's here or not. He might have just passed through."

"But you know he come here?"

"I'm a pretty fair tracker," Miller said. "He came here all right."

"Well, now, Mr. Miller," I said, "I can't have folks, Churkee or not, coming into my town to do no killings. I think you can understand that all right, can't you?"

"Marshal," he said, "I promise you that I won't shoot the man in your town, not unless he forces me to."

"What would you do if you was to see him walk in here right now?" I asked him.

"Well," he said, "I guess I'd run him out of town, and then I'd kill him."

"That's all right, then," I said. "Have another drink."

Chapter Two

Well, hell, I went on and bought that Churkee Indian several more drinks, and I reckon I got him some drunk. I was feeling pretty loose my own self. I thunk that Happy was just about ready to fall over and pass out, and Bonnie was loud and raucous and laughing at ever' little thing that anyone said. Then here come ole Butcher, and when he got to the table, he tossed that sack he had toted with him on the table right in front a' me. I looked up at him, and he was grinning real wide.

"It's empty, Barjack," he said.

"What?" I said. Then it come back to me and I picked up the sack and kindly hefted it. "Oh yeah. That's real good, Butcher. Real good. Set your ass down and have a drink."

Well, the only chair was right next to Miller, and Butcher pulled it out and give Miller a right curious look.

"Miller," I said, "this here is ole Butcher Doyle. He's out from New York City, and he's my other depitty. Butcher, shake hands with Mose Miller, or the Red-Tailed Hawk. He's a goddamned Churkee Indian, and he just hit town up from the Churkee Nation in Indian Territory."

Well, ole Butcher stuck out his hand, and Miller, he tuck it and shuck it, but Butcher never said nothing. He just mostly stared right at Miller.

"A real Indian?" he said final.

"Yes, sir, Mr. Doyle," Miller said.

"I'll have to write Papa about this," Butcher said. "A real Indian."

Aubrey fetched Butcher over a drink, and I waved my glass at him. He had carried along my bottle, and so he went and poured my tumbler full again. Ever'one else was okay, so he went on back to his place at the bar. I was still thinking about that stray Churkee in my town and how come him to be there, but I didn't rightly feel like as if I could quiz him up about it right there in front a' all them folks, so I kept my goddamn mouth shut about it. But I did wonder just who the hell it was he was a-chasing down to kill and what the hell for.

"What kinda six-guns you toting, Miller?" I asked him, mostly to make conversation what would be harmless.

He drawed them both out and handed them over to me butts first. I tuck them and hefted them.

"They're Remingtons," he said, "1888 Model. Forty-fives. They're good shooters."

I give them back to him and hauled out my trusty shooter and handed it over to him.

"I prefer this here Merwin and Hulbert Company forty-five-caliber self-extracting revolver," I said. "I've carried this one here around for a good many years, all except for a time I had to put it in the gunsmith's shop for repair, and then I had to tote around a goddamn Colt."

Miller hefted my shooter in his right hand, then

tossed it over into his left. He spun it around some, first in one hand, then in the other'n. Final he give it back to me.

"It's got a good feel," he said. "I've heard of them, but I've never handled one before. Never even saw one that I know of."

"You'll never handle a better one," I said, as I shoved it back into my holster.

"I'd like to try it sometime," he said.

"Maybe sometime tomorrer," I said. "If that's all right with you."

"Sure thing, Marshal Barjack," Miller said. "I'll be looking forward to it."

"You'll be wanting to buy one for your own self once you try it," I told him. He just kindly laughed at that and tuck hisself another drink. Ole Butcher was a-drinking fast trying to catch up with the rest of us, and whenever his glass went dry on him, he couldn't wait for old Aubrey. He got up and went to the bar to get hisself some more. He was about halfway back to the table when he kindly stopped, looking toward the door, and he called out, "Hey there, Dingle. Barjack, looky here. Here comes ole Dingle."

I turned my head around to get me a look, and sure enough, Dingle was a-coming in and headed right for my table. He was carrying some kind of a package underneath his one arm. When he got to the table, he put the package down and pulled out a chair and set. Butcher got back then, and since Dingle had set his ass down in Butcher's chair, Butcher dragged another chair over from the next table to us and set in it.

"Where you been, Dingle?" he said.

"I just went over to the county seat," said Dingle, "and I caught the mail there a few days early." He went to unwrapping that package he had brung along, and then we could all see that it was a brand-new batch a' books. He tuck one off the top and tossed it to me. I picked it up and looked at it, and there on the cover was a drawing a' me with two guns a-blazing, and on my right-hand side was ole Butcher, and he was shooting too, and on my left was Happy a-blazing away. And then on the far right-hand side was Sly the Widdamaker, and on the far left-hand side was ole Dingle hisself. Dingle handed another copy to Butcher.

"Is that there me?" Butcher said.

"I reckon it is," I said.

"Damn," said Butcher. "I'll have to send this here to my pop."

"I'll give you another one for him," Dingle said.

"Hot damn," Butcher said.

"May I see one of those?" said Miller.

Dingle went and handed him one, and I said, "Oh yeah. Please excuse my rude ass. Mr. Miller, this here is Dingle the Scribbler. He writes books about me. Dingle, shake hands with Mose Miller, the Red-Tailed Hawk, a real Churkee Indian up from Indian Territory."

"Mr. Miller," said Dingle, reaching across in front of Butcher, "it's a pleasure to make your acquaintance."

"Likewise, Mr. Dingle," said Miller. Then he went to thumbing through the pages of Dingle's latest, what was called *Barjack and the Snake-Eyed Gang*. Dingle looked over at Bonnie then.

"Miss Bonnie," he said. "Do you have ink and pen in here somewhere?"

Bonnie yelled out to Aubrey, "Bring us a pen and a ink bottle."

Aubrey brung it over right away, and Dingle went and writ his name underneath his picture on the cover a' one a' them books. Then he give the book and the ink bottle and the pen to Butcher and had him do the same thing. He passed it all around till we had all signed, all that is 'cept for ole Sly what weren't in the place. Then Dingle decided that we all had to sign his whole stack a' books, and we done it. He give a extry copy to Butcher to send to his papa. Butcher couldn't stop a-looking at his picture on the front cover.

"Papa just won't believe this here," he said, more than once.

Just then I heared a familiar voice come from over my shoulder. "Good evening, friends," it said, and I knowed it right away. It were ole Sly, by God. Ever since our last little adventure together a-wiping out that there Snake Eyes Gang, he had tuck to dropping in the Hooch House fairly regular for just one drink with me and whoever else might be in there with me. I reckon we was just too good a' friends for anything like a little animosity from ole Lillian, my ex-wife and his present one, to stand betwixt us.

"Well, howdy, Sly, ole pard," I said. "Pull up a chair and set a spell with us."

Well, he done that, and ole Aubrey, he knowed what Sly wanted, and he brung it right over. Sly thanked him graciously, and then Dingle piped up,

"Mr. Sly, you came just in time." He shoved the whole stack a' books along with the pen and the ink bottle over Sly's way. Sly picked up one book and studied it.

"Not a bad likeness," he said, and then he commenced to signing them, so pretty soon, ole Dingle's books was all signed by all a' the heroes, and he was real goddamn proud. I interduced Sly and Miller and they shuck hands.

Well, I don't know how I done it, but somehow I managed to get my own ass up the stairs with ole Bonnie to our room up above the Hooch House, and whenever I hit the bed I never knowed another damn thing till it was about ten o'clock the next morning. Course, Bonnie was still a-snoozing, and I was real careful not to disturb her rest, knowing how serious she tuck it. I moved around real sneakylike a-getting my ass dressed, and I never bothered her a bit. Then I went slipping outta the room and down the stairs.

Happy was there at my table already, and I was a little surprised to see not just only Butcher but Mose Miller setting there with him. Applewhite was playing cards at his table all by hisself. I think he called it solitude or something like that. I never did play no cards. I figgered it was enough of a gamble just getting through each day and going to bed at night hoping I'd wake up alive in the morning. I headed for my own private table, and ole Aubrey called out to me, "Whiskey or coffee?"

"Both," I said, "and get me a breakfast."

"Right away," he said.

I set down, and I said, "Well, Mr. Miller. I'm a little bit surprised to see you here this morning."

"We were going out to shoot today," he said.

"Oh yeah. That's right," I said. "Well, let me eat first, and then we'll go."

Butcher pulled his British Webley Bulldog pistol outta his pocket and fondled it. "Can I go along?" he said.

"Suit yourself," I said. "I don't give a shit."

Aubrey brung me a cup a' coffee and a tumbler full a' brown whiskey, and he seen that the others' coffee cups was either low or empty, so he went back for the coffeepot and brung it back and refilled them all. I tuck me a good swaller a' whiskey, and all at once, I felt considerable better. Then I went to sipping my coffee. Miller was reading a copy a' Dingle's book. I don't know how he got it away from ole Dingle. I never asked. Pretty soon Aubrey brought out my breakfast, and I et it down in a right hurry. I wiped my mouth off on my coat sleeve, and then I stood up.

"Well," I said, "are we going?"

Miller and Butcher stood up fast, and Happy looked up at me with a face like a goddamn puppy dog.

"Barjack?" he said.

"What?" I snapped back at him.

"You reckon I could come along with you?"

"Oh, hell," I said, "come on along."

We went down to my marshaling office first so I could pick up a few boxes of extry bullets, and then we went to get our horses. Along the way, I seen ole Sly, and I hollered at him. He agreed to go along with us, and we even picked up Dingle. So the six of us rid on outside a' town to a little spot beside the river. I had used this place before as a shooting

range, so there was already a mess a' tin cans and
bottles and such laying around. We set them up on
some big rocks and a fallen log, and then we all
stepped back a distance. I pulled out my Merwin
and Hulbert and handed it to Miller. He hefted it
and done some tricks with it, getting the feel of it.
Then he raised it up and snapped off a shot, bouncing one a' the tin cans off its perch.

"Not bad," I said.

I missed a shot with one a' his Remingtons, and
I grumbled and give it back to him. He give me
back my own shooter, and I fired off three rounds
and hit with each one of them. Happy hit three
cans with six shots, and Butcher hit four out of five
outta his Bulldog. Dingle fired six shots and never
hit nothing he aimed at. Me and ole Miller traded
guns again, and I shot his Remington till I got the
hang of it all right. Sly was just standing by and
watching us. By and by, we was all about shot out,
and then ole Sly stepped up and emptied his two
Colts. He bounced a can with each shot.

The Churkee had loaded up his Remingtons
again, and I guess he had tuck pity on ole Dingle, so
he give him one a' the Remingtons and then commenced to giving him some pointers. And by God,
in just a little while, ole Dingle was hitting about
two or three outta ever' five shots, and he was really
a-beaming too. Miller borried my Merwin and Hulbert once more, and this time he shot up about ten
slugs out of it. He never missed neither. Final he
give it back to me.

"Marshal," he said, "you might be right about
that gun."

"If you want to get yourself one," I said, "I know

where there's one to be had. Only thing is, you might not want to do business with the son of a bitch what has it."

"Why?" said Miller. "Who is it?"

"Name's Henshaw. One a' the two shit-asses what braved you when you come in the Hooch House last night. He's our gunsmith, and he owns the gun shop in town."

"Oh," said Miller. "Well, I might just stop in and have a look at it anyhow."

There was a few more shots fired after that, but mostly we was through. Pretty soon, we mounted up and rid on back into town. Sly went on to Lillian's fancy eating place, and the rest of us went back to the Hooch House. I led the way right back to my own special table, and Aubrey brung me a tumbler a' my special whiskey. The others all ordered what they wanted. We'd been out shooting long enough that it was late enough in the day by then so we was getting some business in the Hooch House by then. There was a cowhand at the bar starting in to get some rowdy, but his pard punched him on the shoulder and give a nod in my direction. The rowdy one looked and calmed down right quicklike. Happy seen it and smiled at me. I give a growl.

"Fellers," I said, "I reckon I better get my ass upstairs and see if my Bonnie sweet pants has woke up yet."

"Be careful, Barjack," Happy said. He knowed real good just how mean and ornery ole Bonnie could be in the morning if she hadn't got all the sleep she thought she needed.

"You want us to do anything while you're gone, boss, uh, Marshal?" Butcher asked.

"Just keep things quiet is all," I said. Then I went on up to the room. I opened the door real easylike and slipped in till I seed that Bonnie was up all right, setting on the edge a' the bed.

"Good morning, sugar tits," I said. "Did you sleep good last night?"

She jumped up and come a-running at me, and when we come together, she woulda knocked me flat on my ass if it weren't for the fact that she wrapped her big arms around me just as her mass hit me.

"I slept just fine, darlin'," she said, "but I missed you whenever I woke up. Where was you?"

"Me and the boys went outta town to do some shooting," I said.

She dragged me back over to the bed and pulled me down on it and went to smooching around on me, and before I knowed it, she had me plumb nekkid, and then she stood up and pulled off her nightygown. She climbed in on top a me, and goddamn, but she like to've killed me. I figgered I must be letting old age catch up with me. I sure as hell couldn't go again. I reckon I mighta disappointed ole Bonnie, but there just weren't nothing for it. I got up and got dressed, and she did too, and then we went on downstairs together. The table was just like it was whenever I had left it.

All the boys stood up for Bonnie when we come to the table. I knowed it weren't for me. Aubrey brung me and Bonnie each a drink. I was tipping back my glass and I caught a glimpse a' Miller, and I seen something in his face. It was mean. He was a-looking toward the front door. I put down my glass and looked around over my shoulder. A man maybe forty years old and wearing a sharp-looking suit had just come through the front doors. I tried to tell if he was wearing a gun or not, but I couldn't see none. I looked at him for just a minute while he walked on up to the bar. Then I looked back at Miller.

"Your man?" I asked him.

"Yes, Marshal," he said. "That's the man all right."

Chapter Three

"Well," I said, "I hope you ain't a-fixing to kill him in here."

"I remember what you said," Miller told me.

Just then that there newcomer glanced over in our direction, and he seed Miller. A kind of a snarl come over his face, and he walked right on over to us where we was setting. He looked right at Miller, and he said, "Siyu, Red-Tailed Hawk."

"I see you too, Cody, you slimy-tailed son of a bitch," Miller said. "Don't try talking Cherokee to me, goddamn you. You don't even know one word."

"You're a long ways from home, Red-Tail," said the one Miller called Cody. "What brings you out this far?"

"I'm trailing a skunk that needs killing," Miller said. "It won't be long now."

"You think not?"

"I'm pretty damn sure."

"You want to make a go of it now?" Cody asked.

"Not here," said Miller. "I promised my friend, Marshal Barjack here, that there wouldn't be any trouble in his town."

"Then I reckon I can just relax while I'm here," Cody said, "and have a few drinks."

"As long as you can pay for them," I said.

"Oh yeah," said Cody. "I'm rolling in dough."

"Go on over to the bar then and have yourself a few snorts," I told him. "Just keep your distance from this here table. We're particular about the smell."

"I'll do that," Cody said. "I can see that Red-Tail has done prejudiced your opinion of me."

He tipped his hat just like as if he was a real gentleman, and he turned and walked off toward the bar, where I could see ole Aubrey poured him a drink and tuck his money. I watched him for a minute or two, and then I said to Miller, "So that there's the scoundrel you're after."

"He's the one," the Churkee said.

"Say," I said, "what was that little exchange you all had right at the start? You know, something about talking Churkee?"

"Oh," said Miller, "he tried to give me a greeting in Cherokee. Properly, it's 'osiyo,' but he said 'see you.'"

"Oh, I get it now," I said. "Say, are you gonna tell me what that son of a bitch done to get you after his ass?"

"Well, I wasn't going to," Miller said, "but you've been a pretty good friend to me, and you are the local law, so I guess I might as well tell it to you. His name is Hiram Cody, but he can't read or write, and calls it 'Harm.' My family had a ranch in the Cooweescoowee District way up north in the Cherokee Nation, up on the Kansas border. Well, Old Harm came in and somehow or other met my baby sister and commenced to courting her. He married her and they settled down on a piece of land way down south, nearly into the Creek Nation, but it didn't take Harm long to find out that farming was hard work. They had two little kids, and he just left them one day. Didn't tell them a thing. Just left. I went down to visit my sister one day, and I found her and the little ones all alone way out in the middle of nowhere with no horse and no food. They were almost starving. They'd have died soon if I hadn't come along when I did. I rode to the nearest store and bought a wagon and a load of food and went back to the house. I got them fed, and then loaded them up and drove them back home. They're living back home on the ranch still. Then one day I heard that Harm was living with another Cherokee woman just a few miles away from the ranch. I felt like he was rubbing it in my face. I rode over to the place where he was supposed to be living meaning to kill him, but he saw me coming and ran away. The woman said that they were married. So I went to the law and signed a paper accusing him of bigamy. They brought him to trial, and he claimed that he was a Cherokee. Said his mama was Cherokee, and his defense was that Cherokee men could have more than one wife. Somehow he got away with it. They let him go, and he left the country. I sat home and seethed about it for a few days, and then I finally decided that I had to track him down and kill him. That's all there was for it, and that's the whole story, except that I followed him here."

"It sounds to me like he's a bastard what sure enough needs killing," I said. "Now, listen here, Mr. Miller. While you was telling that tale, I was thinking through the law, and I was partly mistook before. If you was to kill the son of a bitch outside out in the street in a fair fight, especially if he was to draw first, there wouldn't be no law against that."

I noticed that ole Dingle, what had been real quiet all this time, had hauled out his pocket notebook and was busy scribbling once again. He musta figgered that he had heard the beginnings of another good yarn, and he sure as hell weren't going to let it go by.

"Thanks, Marshal," the Churkee said.

"Just be careful," I said. "I don't want you getting yourself kilt in my town. Hell, then I'd have to go after that goddamned Harm son of a bitch."

"No," Miller said. "I reserve that pleasure for myself."

I noticed that Harm Cody had just ordered hisself another drink, so I figgered there wasn't going to be no action in town real soon. I waved at ole Aubrey, and he brung the bottles to refill ever' one's glasses. I picked mine up and tuck me a good slug out of it. I was kinda looking forward to watching Miller blow away that slimy bastard Harm Cody, and I was actual hoping it would take place right soon. The goddamned snake in the grass couldn't stand there at my bar a-drinking all night long. He'd have to leave sometime, and whenever he did, well, ole Miller could just foller him right out the damn door.

Now, y'all readers might recollect that it had been late morning whenever we come into the Hooch House. Actual it had been close to noon. We had been out a-shooting most a' the morning, and whenever I went up to my room and Bonnie's, ole

Bonnie was just then a-getting outta bed. Then me and her had gone back down and commenced to drinking with the boys, and we had just about drunk up and talked away the rest a' that day. It was evening by this time. Well, that Harm finished up his drink and turned away from the bar. He come a-walking back to my table and a-looking at Miller again.

"You planning to run again, Cody?" Miller asked him.

I noticed that Cody had a couple a' bottles tucked into his coat pockets.

"Looks to me like he is," I said. "He's got a supply a' booze packed for his trip."

"I hate to disappoint you gents," Cody said, "but I'm just going to turn in. I have a camp just out of town, and my partners are waiting for me there. The bottles are for them."

"Get a good night's sleep," said Miller. "You never know when it might be your last."

The asshole tipped his hat and left the place, and I watched him go, and then I went to watching Miller, and for a minute or two, I thunk he was going to get up and foller that Harm Cody out into the street, but he never. He just set there.

"You ain't going to get a better time," I said.

"I'm wondering who his partners are," Miller said, "and just what they might be up to."

"I s'pose that's a good question," I said.

"It can't be any good," Miller said, "and if he didn't lie to us, they're just outside of your town."

"Maybe I had ought to foller him out there and see what can I find out," I said, pushing my chair back.

Miller stood up in a hurry. "Let me do that, Marshal," he said.

I settled back into my chair. "All right," I said.

"Should I ride along with him?" said Happy. It was the first thing he had said in a spell.

"That's a good idea, Happy," I said. "It's about time you had one. Go on."

Miller was damn near out the door, and Happy jumped up and tuck out after him. Butcher got up and follered them as far as the front door, and he stood there a-watching. In a few minutes he come back to the table.

"You didn't want me to go along too, did you, Marshal?" he said.

"If I had I'da said," I told him.

"Yeah," he said. "Well, they rode outta town heading south."

"If that ole boy didn't lie to us," I said, "they ain't very smart. There's better campsites north."

I drained my glass and waved at Aubrey for a refill, and he brung it to me right quicklike. Butcher still had some left in his glass.

"Barjack?" said Bonnie.

"What, sweet ass?" I said.

"Is there going to be trouble?"

"Oh, I don't think I'd call it trouble," I said. "That Churkee is apt to kill him a white man is all, and the way it sounds to me is it sounds like that white man has got it coming. That's all."

I drunk me a couple more drinks, and it was late enough that the crowd was a-clearing out. There was just us and a few customers left in the place. Applewhite put his cards away and was fixing to shut down for the night. I still had me about a half a tumbler a' good whisky, and I think I knowed better, but I picked up that glass and rared back so far that I was just balancing on the two back legs a' my chair, and I drained that glass, but whenever I done it, I fell on over bass-ack'ards and hit my head on the floor whenever I landed. I heared ole Bonnie through the fog as she squealed, "Barjack," but I never answered. I just laid there.

"Butcher," she said. "You and Dingle haul him up to my bed."

"It would sure be easier, ma'am," I heared Dingle answer, "to carry him down to the jail than to tote him up the stairs."

"No," she said, "I want him in my bed. Oh, hell, never mind."

My eyes was half open. I wasn't out cold. And I seed ole Bonnie get up outta her chair, and then I seed her bend over me. Well, what I really seen was I seed her massive big tits come close to my face whenever she bent over me, and the next thing I knowed was I felt her take a holt a' me and heave me up and over her shoulders. It was kind of a shock, but I managed to keep on a-playing like as if I was out cold, and then she walked on over to the stairs and started in to climbing them. I could tell when she reached the top and walked down the hallway, and I sure as hell knowed when she tossed my ass onto the bed. She pulled off my boots, and then she went to undressing me. It weren't long till I was for sure out cold. I never knowed nothing else till I come to in the morning, and it was so late that Bonnie had done got up and got her ass all dressed for the day.

I stirred a little bit and set up on the side a' the bed a-holding my head in my hands, and I guess I moaned a little bit. Bonnie come a-running and hugged the hell outta me.

"Oh, Barjack, sweetness," she said, "are you feeling all right?"

"Hell, yes," I said. "I'm just fine. A-raring to go. What time a' day is it anyhow?"

"I don't know, darlin'," she said. "I reckon it's near noon."

It come into my head then where Miller and Happy had went the night before, and I shoved her loose a' me and stood up. "I got to get dressed and go down," I said.

"All right, honey," she said. "Take it easy. I'll help you."

She dressed me in a clean suit a' clothes and final set my hat on my head, but she set it on crookedy, and I straightened it up. Then I headed for the door. When I was on my way down the stairs, I seed Happy and Miller and Butcher a-setting at my table. I went on over there and joined them.

"Morning, Marshal," Miller said.

"Howdy, Barjack," said Happy. "It ain't really morning no more."

"Never mind all that," I said, and then I looked right into the face a' that Churkee. "Did you kill anyone last night?" I asked him.

"No, sir, I didn't," Miller said.

Aubrey come to the table just then and set me down a tumbler a' whisky and a cup a' hot coffee. I tuck me a sip a' the whisky first, and of a sudden, I felt some better. Then I had me a sip a' that hot coffee.

"All right then," I said. "Tell me about last night."

Both of them started in to talking at the same time. "Just hold it," I said. "One at a time."

They looked at each other, and then Happy give Miller a nod. "We followed Harm a little ways south out of town," he said, "and sure enough, he came to a campsite. There were four other men there waiting for him. He took out a bottle, opened it, and passed it around. Me and Happy dismounted and slipped up as close as we dared, but we couldn't hear them very well."

"But they was scheming something up, Barjack," Happy said. "Way out there the way they was, they set real close together and talked low, and ever' now and then, that ole Harm feller would pick up a stick and draw something in the dirt."

"Well," said Miller, "they finally quit talking and turned in for the night, and we left and came back to town. I thought we'd better tell you about it rather than take a chance on killing Cody with those other four men there."

"Good thinking," I said. "Likely you'da just got yourself kilt. Maybe Happy too. So they was scheming on something, was they? I imagine that Cody was a-planning your murder and showing them the lay of the town is what they was doing. You'd best watch your ass from here on."

"Don't worry about me," Miller said.

"Them other four," I said. "Did you rekernize them?"

"Not me," said Happy. "They was strangers for sure."

"I've never seen them before," said Miller.

"So he's picked them up along the way after he

left outta the Churkee Nation," I said. "Well, we'll be ready for them all right."

"Barjack," said Miller. "Let me show you what I got this morning." And he reached down and hauled out a six-shooter and laid it on the table, shoving it toward me. It was a Merwin and Hulbert self-extracting .45, just like mine. I picked it up and hefted it. It felt good, just like mine. I grinned and handed it back to him.

"That's a fine one," I said.

"I went down to the gun shop this morning first thing," Miller said. "That ole boy, Henshaw, was none too happy to see me, and he sure didn't want to serve me, but he was glad enough to have my money. So I bought it. Then I rode back out to where we went to shoot and tried it out a little. It's a good shooter."

"Well, by God," I said, "I'm glad you got it. You won't never be sorry." And I thunk about him a-using it on that damned Harm, but I didn't say nothing about that. Instead I just said, "Keep it handy. You just might have a need for it afore long."

Chapter Four

Well, I had been asleep for a while that next night, and as I recall, I had been having some good dreams. It seems like as if the better the dreams, the more likely they will get interrupted. My own perticler dreams that night was doubling up the sweet times I had in bed with Ole Bonnie. I don't reckon I should try to tell you just where I was at in my sweet dream whenever I was rudely awoke by the goddamned blast. But I can tell you that it shuck my bed whenever it went off. I can also tell you that it brung me straight up a-setting up in bed, and most likely my eyes was wide-open too. It brung ole Bonnie up the same way, and me and her looked right into each other's face. Her eyes was for sure wide-open.

"Barjack," she said, "what the hell was that?"

"Goddamned if I know," I said, scrambling out of bed, "but I better by God find out."

I was plumb outta bed then and pulling on my britches. Bonnie actual got up and fetched me my boots, and I pulled them on. She handed me my six-gun and rig and I strapped that on right quick. Then I headed for the door, and as I was a-jerking it open, Bonnie slapped my hat down on my head. I got my

old ass downstairs more faster than you would believe, and I hustled it on out the front door and into
the street. There was a couple of cowboys out there
ahead a' me, and I seed ole Henshaw out there too.
It didn't take long to figger out where the blast had
come from, on account a' the smoke was visible. It
was down at the bank. I went to running toward the
bank, and so did ever'one else what was out on the
street.

Whenever I come up close to the bank's front
door, ole Happy come up beside me. He was only
half dressed, like me, too. I give him a look, and
I said, "Come on, Happy." We went through that
front door. Smoke was thick inside, and I went to
making my way toward where it was thickest, and
pretty damn soon we found ourselves standing in
front a' the big vault, which had obvious been
blowed open. There wasn't no one inside the bank
no more. "Happy," I said, "go find Mr. Golden and
bring him here in a hurry."

"Yes, sir," said Happy, and he tuck off. Peester
come up beside me just then, still in his nightshirt,
and ole Butcher come up on the other side a' me.

"Somebody robbed the bank," said Peester.

"That's a brilliant observation, Pisster," I said.

"What do we do, Barjack?" asked Butcher.

"Just stick close to me," I said.

There was a small fire what the blast had caused
a-growing up around the wall behind the blowed-
open vault, and I headed back out onto the street.
I noticed on my way out that the crooks had broke
the glass outta the front door winder. Butcher
follered me. There was a pretty good sized crowd
gathered around by this time, and I hollered out

for some a' the men to form up a bucket brigade and sop out that fire inside. They got it going right quick. Then I seed Happy hurrying back and bringing along Golden, the banker, with him. They come right up to me.

"What's happened?" Golden said.

"Someone broke into your bank and blowed open your vault," I said. "I want you to go in there and tell me just what's missing."

"Yes, sir," he said, and he went on in.

I helt up my arms trying to quiet down the crowd, and it tuck a few minutes, but they final did hush up some.

"I want to know," I yelled out, "if anyone here seed anything what might help us out here."

Folks looked down at the goddamned street and muttered things like, "I was asleep and the blast woke me up."

"I didn't see nothing."

"Me neither."

Then I seen ole Jacobsen, what was kinder our town drunk, a-working his way through the crowd and moving toward me.

"Let him through there," I said, and the crowd kinder moved to two sides, and Jacobsen come on through. "You got something to say to me, Jake?" I ast him.

"I seen them, Marshal," he said.

"Where was you?" I said.

He jerked his thumb toward a spot across the street. "I was sleeping right over there on the sidewalk," he said. "I had just come awake, and I was wanting another drink real bad. I don't know what time it was, but I knowed that it was way into the nighttime, and then five men come a-riding into town. I remember thinking that it was kinder strange for five men to come a-riding in that time a' night."

"So what'd you do?" I ast him.

"I just huddled down to keep me outta sight," he said. "They got off their horses. One man stayed with them and held the reins. The other ones all went to the bank. They busted the glass and went inside. Well, I knowed then that they was bank robbers."

"Well, now," I said, "that was plenty smart a' you, Jake. Go on."

"Well, it was quiet then for a couple a' minutes, and then come that awful explosion. It was quiet again for another couple a' minutes, and then I seen the four come out. One of them was toting a sack. They mounted up and rode off in a hurry."

"Which way did they go?" I said.

He pointed off to the south, and said, "They went outta town that way, Marshal."

"Headed south, huh?" I said.

"Did I help you out, Marshal Barjack?" he said.

"Hell, yes, Jake. You done yourself proud. From now on, anytime you need to pass out or just go to sleep, you feel free to lay your ass down on the sidewalk on Main Street. And whenever the Hooch House opens up in a while, you go in there and tell ole Aubrey that I said to give you all the drinks you want."

"All I want?" he said.

"That's what I said, and I meant it." I looked around till I seed ole Happy, and I said to him, "Happy, get our horses ready to ride."

"Yessir."

"Hell, get three," I said.

"Yes, sir," he said, and he hustled his ass off.

"I'll get my own," said Miller, suddenly appearing outta the crowd. He turned and rushed off, and then ole Sly come a-walking up.

"I'll get mine too," he said, "if you'll allow me to ride along."

"You're goddamn welcome, Widdamaker," I said. "Let's meet in front a' my marshaling office."

Golden come back outta the bank just then, and he come up to me. "Barjack," he said, "they cleaned us out, all except for a small amount of cash in one of the tellers' drawers."

The bucket brigade had just about come to a halt by then. I looked back inside, and I could see that the fire was out. The place was still full a' smoke. I went back out and run smack into Bonnie.

"Barjack," she said. "They rob the bank?"

"Cleaned it out," I said.

"What're you fixing to do?"

"Take a posse and ride after the sons a' bitches."

"Be careful, sweetness," she said. "Don't get hurt."

"Worry about them robbers," I said. "I mean to bring back their hides."

"And our money," said Golden, who was still standing by.

"Don't you worry none about that neither," I said to him. "Some of it's my money and Bonnie's. We'll get it back all right."

Bonnie was still hanging on to me real tight whenever I started in to walking toward my marshaling office, and she went all the way down there

with me. When we come close to the office, I seed
that the Churkee was already there, mounted up
and ready to ride. We walked on up, and I seed that
he was a-wearing his two Remington revolvers and
had his new Merwin and Hulbert shooter tucked
in his belt. He had a rifle in his saddle boot that
looked to me to be a Henry, but I didn't really see it
all that good. I went on into the office and got me a
good Winchester rifle, and I commenced to stuffing
all my pockets with boxes a' bullets. When I stepped
back outside, I handed a couple a' boxes to Miller,
and I seed Sly come riding up. I give him some extry ammunition. Happy was riding down the street
leading two saddled horses. When he come up to
office, I got on one and Butcher climbed aboard the
other one. We was ready to go, but then here come
ole Dingle riding up real fast.

"Wait for me," he shouted.

"You got a gun, Scribbler?" I ast him.

"No, sir," he said, "but—"

"Here, Dingle," said Miller, handing over one a'
his Remingtons. Then he tuck the Merwin and Hulbert outta his belt and holstered it where that Remington had been. I pulled out a box a' shells and
handed it to Dingle.

"All right," I said. "Let's get on our way."

I led the way outta town and my five-man posse
follered me. We hadn't got far before we heared
someone riding up behind us. I slowed down and
looked over my shoulder and seed Henshaw and
Martin coming up fast. When they come close,
Henshaw called out, "We're riding with you."

"Well, come along then," I said.

We rid along a ways when Happy pointed off the road and said, "Right over there was their camp, Barjack."

We hadn't give voice to it yet, but I reckon that we all knowed we was trailing Harm Cody and his four pals. We moved on down to the campsite, and the Churkee dismounted to look around. Final he looked up at me.

"Well?" I said.

"I'd say they broke camp before they rode into town. They've been gone from here for a while."

"Can you tell us where they went from town?" I ast him.

"They kept going south on this road," he said.

"Let's ride," I said. And I never waited. I turned my horse and headed on. The others were right behind me. Miller come up last, on account a' he had to get his ass mounted up again. But he caught up again real quick and was riding right along beside a' me. He was watching the trail we was a-follering. By and by, he said, "They've slowed down now."

"Saving their horses, I reckon," I said. "They've rid them hard for a time now. How much of a lead do you reckon they have on us?"

"I'd say they're a couple of hours ahead," Miller said.

"Let's ride hard for a ways," I said, and I kicked up my ole horse. The rest all done the same to keep up with me. We rid along that way for a few miles before I slowed us down again. My ole horse was a-panting. "We any closer to them?" I ast ole Miller.

"Not much," he said.

We kept on a-plodding along our way. Once or trwice I ast him if we still on their trail for sure, and he assured me that we was. So I just kept on a-going. Then we come to a fork in the road, and ole Miller, he hauled back on his reins and stopped his horse. "Hold on," he said.

"What is it?" I said.

"One of them turned off here by himself," Miller said. "The other four kept going straight."

"What the hell?" I said. "One of them off by his-self?"

"That don't make no sense, Barjack," Happy said then.

"So who do we follow?" said Butcher.

"There ain't no way for us to know who it is," I said.

"It could be any one of them," said Miller. "Even Cody himself."

"Maybe a couple of us ought to go after that one," said Henshaw. "What do you say, Barjack?"

Well, I tuck me a minute to think it all over, and it come to me that I could send off Martin and Henshaw. I didn't like having them along in the first place, but then I didn't trust them off by their own selfs neither. Final I looked over at ole Sly.

"Sly," I said, "what would you say if I was to ask you to take ole Henshaw there and foller that lone wolf?"

Sly looked at Henshaw and then he looked back at me. "I'd say all right," he answered.

"Henshaw?" I said.

Henshaw looked at his buddy Martin and then at Sly. Final he looked at me. "You're the boss here, Barjack," he said. "Whatever you say is all right with me."

"Okay," I said. "You two go on after that one.

The rest of us will stay on the trail of the other four. Good luck to you."

"The same to you," said Sly, and he turned off the main road to foller that lone wolf. I set and watched them go for a few seconds, and then I said, "Let's get after them other ones." I started in to ride and the other'ns follered me. As we rid along, I was a-thinking about what I had did to ole Sly. I didn't have no high opinion a' Henshaw atall, but if I had to split up my posse, it figgered that Sly was the onlyest one what I could really trust. I counted on him to do whatever it was that needed to be did, and if that goddamned Henshaw failed to back him up properlike, well, what the hell, Sly was the least likely one of all of us to need any help. He'd be all right. I tried to put him outta my mind.

"Them tracks saying anything to you, Miller?" I ast.

"Not much," he said. "They're just moving ahead is all."

"Well, at least we know that we're still on their goddamned trail," I said.

"Wait a minute," Miller said. "They've picked up their pace again. Moving along pretty fast now."

"Let's keep up with them," I said, and I spurred my horse up. The others did the same thing. We kept it up for maybe two miles, and I slowed us down then. Up ahead was a little trail heading off to our left, what woulda been east, and Miller hauled up again a-studying the trail. He pointed down that little lane.

"One of them went down there," he said.

"What?" said Butcher. "Again?"

"I'm not thinking for them," Miller said. "Just watching their tracks."

"I'll be goddamned," I said. I shoved my hat back and went to scratching my head.

Chapter Five

Well, I went to wondering just what the hell was a-going on with those bastards, splitting up like that, but what was worse, it was causing me to split up my own forces too damn much. There weren't no way a' knowing just which ones a' them outlaws was splitting off down them side roads, nor who mighta been carrying the loot. I didn't see how I could ignore any one a' them neither. I was tempted to lead the whole lot a' what I had left with me after that one, but then if the main bastard Cody and the bank loot was still headed south ahead of us, we'd lose time that way. I had to split us up some more. I couldn't see no way around it. I looked around at each a' the remaining members a' my little posse. Final I heaved a big, heavy sigh.

"Happy," I said, "you take Dingle and foller this son of a bitch."

"Okay, Barjack," Happy said, and he didn't wait no time. He just turned his horse onto that there trail and lit out. Ole Dingle hustled his animal around to foller like as if he was about to be left behind.

"All right," I said, "let's the rest of us get going," and I whipped up my ole black stallion. The three

men left all follered me. Miller stayed right up aside
a' me where he could read the trail we was a-going
after. They was four of us left, me and Miller and
Butcher and that ole Martin, and we was on the trail
of three owl hoots. We didn't know if that Cody was
one a them or not, and we didn't have no idee what
the hell they was up to.

I couldn't help myself. As I rid along the road I
kept a-wondering how them that I split off from my
posse was a-doing. I weren't worried none about
ole Sly and not too much about Happy, but I just
couldn't keep myself from wondering about them. I
wondered, did they catch up with them bastards
yet, and then if they had, did they kill them or
what? And I wondered if either one a' them was
Cody, and did whoever they was have the money
or any part of it along with them? I tried to stop
thinking thattaway, but I just couldn't help myself. I
tried to think about who it was up ahead of us, but
that didn't make no difference neither. The Churkee final interrupted my thoughts, for which I was
some thankful.

"Barjack," he said, "we're narrowing the gap. I'd
say they're no more than an hour ahead of us now."

We'd been moving along kinda easy to save our
horses, so I said, "Let's pick up the pace somewhat,"
and we went to running our critters. In a few more
minutes, we come to a place where the road nar-
rowed a bit and it had tall hills on both sides. I
shoulda knowed better, and I could still kick my
own self in the ass if I was agile enough for it, but
I just only kept right on a-racing along that damn
road. Then of a sudden they was shots fired, and I
heared one a' them whistle right beside my ear.

"Goddamn it," I shouted. "Demount and take cover."

We all went to getting down off our horses and running for the side a' the road and hunting cover. But I seed ole Martin, while he was a-running, take a slug in his leg. He yelled and stumbled and fell down in the middle a' the road a-bleeding like a stuck pig. Miller run back out in the road and grabbed him under his arms and dragged him to the roadside and behind a big rock that was a-setting there real convenient-like. The bullets kept on a-splatting all around us. One of our horses went down a-screaming with blood pouring outta his neck.

Me and what was left a' my posse was busy sweeping our eyeballs acrost them high hills and looking for whoever it was what was taking pot-shots at us. Final I seed some smoke puffs about halfway up the side a' the hill on the other side a' the road from where I was slunked down behint a bush. I commenced to squinnying my eyeballs up on that hillside where I seed them the puffs a' smoke, but I couldn't for the life a' me locate no goddamn shooter up there. Then one a' the outlaws popped up from behind a rock up there and tuck a shot that hit the dirt just to my right-hand side.

I yiked out loud, and Miller the Churkee, what had managed to get off a' his horse with his rifle gun, snapped off three shots real quicklike and that owl hoot up there jerked and screamed and went and fell down the hillside for a few feet. He sure as hell looked like as if he was kilt. Then a whole damned barrage follered, and I laid my ass down flat on the ground. I suspect ever'one else done the same thing. Then the shots quit, and it got awful quiet for a spell, and then I heared some hoofbeats off in the distance. We all waited for some time, and nothing more happened atall.

At long last I stood up real slow, and still nothing happened. "Get up, ever'one," I called out. "They've rid off." The rest a' my posse come up to their feet, and still no one shot at us, so I guessed that I was exact right in my judgment. Well, ole Martin, he never stood up. He was a-laying behint that rock where Miller dumped him, and he was a-moaning and a-groaning. I walked right past him on my way out into the road, and I seed that his leg was a-bleeding pretty bad.

"Someone see can you stop that bleeding," I said, and Miller went over to see what he could do. Then I looked up on the side a' that hill. "Who wants to climb up that there hillside and locate that one body?"

"I'll go, Barjack," Butcher said.

"Take on off then," I said, and ole Butcher went to running up the hillside. He slipped and fell down a couple a' times on his way, but he final got there, and I seed him look around some and then and head on back down. He slipped down again a couple more times, but he did make it down and out into the road, and told me that there weren't no body.

I shook my head, and then I turned back toward ole Miller, who was still a-messing around with Martin, and I said, "That one what was shot got away."

"Barjack," Miller said, "I did the best I could here, but if we don't get this man to a doctor, he's liable to bleed to death."

"Well, goddamn it," I said. "If we take the time to go back, Cody and them others'll get away clean."

"He can't last," Miller said.

I knowed how bad Miller wanted to get that damned Cody, so I knowed it were a sacrifice for him to say what he done. "Well," I said, "someone put Ole Martin into a saddle, and then let's all mount up."

"Which way are we going, Marshal?" said Butcher.

"Back to Asininity," I said, "quick time."

Miller and Butcher heaved ole Martin up into a saddle, and Martin damned near howled with the pain. We had one kilt horse, so that meant we was short one. Miller got up behint Martin so he could hold him up straight in the saddle, and we headed back. Martin moaned all the damn way. I most near wished he would just go on ahead and die, but he never. I could see that blood was still a-dripping from his leg wound.

We had to slow down pretty quick so as to save our mounts, and we was just a-plugging along without no one a-saying nothing, just ole Martin groaning and whimpering. It come to me that he was being nursemaided by the same man that him and his buddy Henshaw had tried to pick a fight with in the Hooch House, and I wondered if he thunk anything atall about that. I kinda doubted it on account a' all his caterwauling. I figgered he weren't thinking about nothing but his own damn misery.

Like I said, we was plodding along, and then I seed ole Happy and ole Dingle the Scribbler come a-riding into the road up ahead of us. They seed us a-coming and stopped to wait for us. Whenever we caught up to them, ole Happy, he said, "What's going on, Barjack?"

"Ole Martin got his ass shot up," I said. "We're taking him in to the doc."

"You letting that Cody and them others get away?" he said.

"Hell," I said, "Miller said Martin'd bleed to death if he didn't get to a doc right quick."

"Oh," said Happy.

"I guess you didn't have any choice then," said Dingle.

"I reckon not," I said. "Now tell me. What the hell are you doing back here?"

"We run into a dead end," said Happy. "We follered that trail for a few miles till we come to a old shack, and then we dismounted and sneaked up to it. We never heared nothing. Final, I bursted in through the front door. Well, it was the only door, but only there weren't no one in there. We nosed around some outside, and it looked to me like as if the son of a bitch we was after had went and cut acrost the hills a-heading back for the main road to join back up with his buddies. I decided we should just ought to come back to the road and see could we catch up with you."

I didn't say nothing for a space. We just continued riding slowlike toward Asininity. Then final I said, "It looks to me like Cody sent them two off just to get me to split up the posse the way I done. The sorry-ass son of a bitch. It looks like he outsmarted me all right."

"Aw, there wasn't no way you could know, Marshal," Happy said.

I noticed outta the corners a' my eyeballs that ole

Dingle had pulled out his little notebook and was a-scribbling in it. I never said nothing about it, though. Martin howled out in pain like as if something had just hurted him real bad. I decided we could pick up the pace, and so I tole ever'one, and we headed on faster. We had rid on ahead maybe a mile or so when I happened to glance over and see that Martin had apparently passed out. Miller was a-holding him up in the saddle. We went on going fast for another mile or so, and then I slowed us down again.

I was pissed off that ole Martin had went and got hisself shot, making us have to turn around and go back. I was thinking that had been mighty small minded a' him to do that. It didn't make no sense, me thinking like that, a-thinking that he had damn near did it a purpose. I can say that now, but at the time I was for sure pissed off at him for it.

About the time we had slowed down, I seed ole Sly the Widdamaker ride out onto the road up ahead and right behint him come Henshaw. Henshaw was a-leading a horse that looked to have a body throwed over it. We come to a halt whenever we got up to them.

"What you got there, Widdamaker?" I ast.

"We caught up with him, Barjack," Sly said, "and he wouldn't come along peacefully."

"Well," I said, "it looks to me like as if you taught him better. We're headed back on account of ole Martin there got his ass shot and is like to bleed to death."

Then ole Sly, he raised up his left hand, and he had a bag in it.

"Is that there the money?" I ast him.

"I don't know if it's all of it," he said, "but it's a bagful."

"Well, I be goddamned," I said.

"Barjack," said Miller, "we'd better be going."

I looked over at him a-hanging on to Martin there, and I said, "Okay." Then I started in to riding again, and the rest rid along with me. There wasn't nothing more to tell about the ride the rest a' the way back into Asininity on account a' nothing of any interest tuck place. We moved along as fast as we could, slowing down ever' now and then for the sake a' the horses.

When we final come back to town, it was already after dark, and we rid straight up to the front of ole Doc Cutter's place, and I told Butcher to help Miller get Martin down and into the doc's place. Whilst they was a-getting Martin down, I demounted and went up to the door and banged on it real loud a-hollering at the same time. "Doc," I yelled out. "Doc, get your ass up and open the door." I kept it up till he come to the door and opened it. By then Butcher and Miller had Martin up to the door too.

"What the hell is it?" Doc said.

"Martin's shot and bleeding," I said.

"Well, bring him on in," said Doc.

Butcher and Miller went to carrying him in, and I said, "I'll be over to the Hooch House," and I left them there to deal with the wounded man. I rid my horse on over to the Hooch House, and the others went along with me. Sly carried that bag into the place and we all set down around my personal table. Aubrey seed us coming and brung us all drinks, and ole Bonnie like to knocked me over running up to me and slapping her fat arms around me.

"Oh, Barjack," she said. "I been so worried about you. God, I'm glad you're back."

"Oh, hush up, Bonnie," I said, "and let's set down."

Well, she hushed and we set. I picked up my tumbler full a' whiskey and had me a nice long drink, and then it come to me that after all, I was just as glad that ole Martin had got hisself shot and brung us back to town. Sly plopped that bag a' money on the table in front a' me, and I looked at it, and I said, "Happy, fetch the banker in here."

"Yes, sir," he said, and he jumped up and run. Dingle was a-scribbling again. "Barjack," he said, "are we going back after them in the morning?"

"Hell," I said, "I don't really see no reason to do that. Sly kilt one of them, and we got the money back."

"But the others are still guilty of bank robbery," he said.

I looked up and scowled, and Sly said, "Dingle's right, Barjack."

I was saved on account a' Happy come back in just then with the banker, and I open up that sack and dumped it out on the table in front a' me. The ole money-grubber's eyes opened up real wide when he seen it.

"Count it," I said, and he set down and went to counting. Whenever he was did, I said, "Well, is it all there?"

"Yes, sir," he said. "You got it all. That's wonderful."

"Well," I said, "what ain't so wonderful is that we only got one a' the goddamned outlaws."

"You got one outlaw," the moneylender said, "and you brought all the stolen money back. I'd say you did real well, and I believe everyone in town will agree with me."

I didn't want to deal with him no more, and I said, "Get that money back into the bank." He stuffed it back into the sack and tuck it outta the place with him. "Well," I said, "that's that. By the way, Sly, what the hell did you do with that stiff?"

"I dropped it off in front of the undertaker's parlor," he said. "Just hitched the horse outside."

"Did you tell anyone?" I ast him.

"No. I figured he'd find it in the morning when he opens the place up."

"Well, hell," I said, "I reckon you're right about that. Still, I expect we had ought to tell him about it. Happy, you run over and wake him up and tell him."

"Yes, sir," Happy said, and like before, he jumped up and run outta the place. It come to me that I was sure as hell lucky to have ole Happy for a depitty, but I damn sure weren't going to tell him that. I finished off my whiskey and waved the empty glass in the air, and ole Aubrey come real quick with my bottle and poured it full again. Bonnie got up and went to the bar for her refill, and I watched her various parts a-bouncing all over the place as she went. She sure was ample. Sly finished his one drink and stood up.

"I'd better be getting along," he said.

Bonnie had just came back to the table with her fresh drink, and she said, "Good night, Mr. Sly," and several of the others around the table said something like that to him. I kinda grunted is all I done. Sly touched the brim a' his black hat and walked on outta the place.

"Barjack," said Dingle, "you never did answer the question of whether or not we're going after the robbers again."

"I been thinking on it," I said, "and it come to me that they're way outta my jurisdiction. I'm just only a town marshal is all, you know. What I can do is I can send wires to all the towns south of us to look out for the bastards."

"I'll be going after them," said Miller, "at least one of them."

"That there is your right and your privilege," I said, and I drained my glass and helt it up for Aubrey to see. It come into my head then that I had ever' intention a' getting my ass good and drunk that night.

Chapter Six

Well, hell, I slept purty late the next morning, and I woked up in my own bed. I ain't got no idee who put me in it, and to tell you the truth I didn't really give a damn neither. I slept so damn late that ole Bonnie was even up and gone. She weren't nowhere in the room. Well, I set up kinda slowlike and helt my head in my hands for a spell and rubbed my eyes somewhat. Final I stood up and kinder staggered across the room to where a bowl a' water set on a table, and I splashed my face in it a bit. Then I dried me off with a towel. I got my ass dressed kinda slow, and the last thing I done was I strapped on my Merwin and Hulbert self-extracting revolver and then put my hat on my head. I walked outta the room and down the stairs.

Bonnie was a-setting at my table with Butcher and Happy, and ole Dingle was even there. Aubrey had me a drink and a cup a' coffee there by the time I set my ass down. Bonnie said, "Thanks, Aubrey," I reckon on account a' she knowed that I weren't about to say nothing atall to him. I tuck me a big slug a' that wonderful stuff, and I felt some better all of a sudden. Then I went to sipping that hot coffee. I looked up and around, and I realized that someone was missing. Then it come into my mind real slow that I didn't see no Churkee around nowhere.

"Say," I said, "where's that damn Churkee at?"

"Miller?" said Happy.

"Yeah, sure," I said, "that Churkee Mose Miller. Who the hell else? You know any other Churkees in town?"

"Well, no," said Happy. "I sure don't."

"Well," I said, "where the hell is he?"

"Oh," Happy said, "why, he rode out a' town early this morning."

"He rid out early?" I said. "Where the hell'd he go?"

"He went out after that feller."

"That Cody?" I said.

"Yeah. That one. Cody. He went after him."

"Goddamn it," I said, slapping my hat down on the table and nearly spilling my drink. I never spilt it, though. Instead I picked it up and took a good long drink. I thunk about what I had said about it taking me outta my jurisdiction to go after him, and I coulda kicked my own ass if I was still able to do it. I didn't like the idee a' Churkee going after that son of a bitch all by his lonesome. I got to tell you, I had went and tuck a liking to that fool Indi'n. "Did anyone go with him?" I ast.

"No, sir," said Happy, "He went out all by his lonesome."

"Well, shit," I said. I stood up and paced around a bit.

"Are we going after him?" Happy ast me.

I didn't answer him right away. I was kinder wanting to go after him. That Cody still had him three pards as far as I could tell. But it really was outta my jurisdiction. After all, I was only the town marshal a' Asininity. And he had a good start on me, and that Cody even had a better one. "No," I said. "Hell, no, we ain't going after him. We ain't going nowhere."

Just then that goddamned pettifogging Peester come walking into the Hooch House, and he come right back to my table. I set back down to my whiskey and my coffee. Peester walked back and stuck out his hand for me to shake, but I ignored it.

"Congratulations, Barjack," he said. "That was a great job you did yesterday."

"What the hell you talking about, shyster?" I said.

"Why, getting that outlaw and bringing back the bank money, of course. You did a great job."

"Oh, that," I said. I never bothered to mention that it were Sly what done it all. "Hell, it's just all part a' the job, Mayor."

"Well, we're all real proud of you, Marshal," Peester said.

"Yeah, yeah."

"Well, uh, I'll be in my office if you need me for anything," he said, and he turned and walked back outta the place. I damn near said, "What the hell would I need you for?" but I never. For once I kept my damned mouth shut. Bonnie musta been thinking the same thing. She smiled at me real sillylike and patted me on the arm. I felt like smacking her one, but I never done that neither. Hell, I knowed better. She could hit harder than me.

"Barjack," she said. "You're a hero again."

"I ain't no hero," I said.

"Yes," she said. "You damn sure are."

"Aw, sugar tits," I said, "I don't want to talk about it no more."

She hugged me real tight and said, "All right, sugar. We won't talk about it no more, but you are a hero."

"All right," I said. "All right."

"You're my hero." And she smacked me on the side a' my face with a real wet, sloppy kiss. When she pulled away from me, I wiped the slobber off my skin. Then I picked up my tumbler and tuck me another drink.

"Your coffee's going to get cold," she said.

I picked up the cup and tuck a sip, and it was already kinder lukewarm, I made a face and put the cup down. "It ain't quite cold," I said.

"It's tepid then," said Dingle.

"Tepid?" I said. "What the hell does that mean? Tepid."

"Well," said Dingle, "it means kind of lukewarm. You know, cooled off but not yet cold. Tepid."

"Tepid," I said. I kinder liked the sound a' that word. "Tepid."

I tuck up the cup again and dranked down the rest a' the tepid coffee. Then I had me another drink a' whiskey. I emptied the glass on that one, and ole Aubrey started over with my bottle, but I waved him back to the bar and stood up.

"Where you going, Barjack?" Bonnie said.

"Over to my marshaling office," I said. "I got some paperwork to do."

"Well, don't go nowhere else without telling me first," she said.

"I ain't going nowhere else, cute ass," I said. I

walked on out onto the sidewalk and headed for the marshaling office, and I swear to God, ever'one I passed on the street slapped me on the back and said, "Congratulations, Marshal," or "Good job, Barjack," or some such trash. I just grumbled at the first couple of them. After that I just kept on a-walking and didn't even let on I heared them. When I come to the marshaling office, I fetched myself my bottle and poured me a glassful. I had dranked down about half of it when ole Doc Cutter come into the office. I looked up.

"Howdy, Doc," I said.

"Barjack," said Doc. "Martin's dead. I just thought you'd want to know."

"Dead?" I said. "Hell, he was just shot in the goddamned leg is all."

"He lost a lot of blood before you got him to me," Doc said, "and he still had the bullet in his leg. He likely got some lead poisoning. Anyhow, he's gone."

"Well, I be goddamned," I said. "Set your ass down, Doc, and have a drink."

By God he did, and I found another glass and poured him one. He tuck a healthy sip.

"Well," he said, "you got one of them anyway. One for one. That makes it even."

"Even ain't what I aim for, Doc," I said. "There's four more of them bastards, and I ain't sure which one of them shot ole Martin. I do know who was the ringleader, though, and he's still loose out there somewheres. There's four more lawbreakers out loose, and they needs to be in jail or kilt. No. I ain't satisfied with one for one."

"No," Doc said, "I guess not."

Now, I had done been thinking on this ever' since I had heared about Churkee riding out all by his lonesome that morning, but this little bit a' converse with ole Doc made me think about it even harder and more specific. I was absolute damned ashamed a' my own self for letting that Cody and his pals ride off, even without the bank money. It come to me that I had got to do something, and I got up right then and walked out, leaving Doc with what was left a' his whiskey, and I went right on over to ole Peester's office. It kinder startled him whenever I barged in.

"Peester," I said, "I got to talk to you."

Well, he calmed hisself down, and then he said, "What is it, Barjack?"

"What does the law say about me leaving outta my jurisdiction to chase after them goddamned bank robbers?"

"Well, I—I'm not sure," he said. "You could take a leave from your job and go out as a bounty hunter, I guess."

"A goddamned bounty man?" I said.

"Wait a minute," he said, and he turned around and pulled a big fat book off a shelf behind him. He put that book on his desk and went to thumbing through it, and when he come to a certain page, he went to reading it over. Then he looked up at me. "Barjack," he said, "as long as you're pursuing someone who committed a crime in your town, you can go after him."

"The son of a bitch robbed our bank," I said.

"You can go after him," said Peester. "It's all right. It's legal."

"That's all I need to know," I said, and I turned around and left outta his office and headed right back to the Hooch House. Happy and Butcher was both still setting at my table with ole Bonnie. So was Dingle. I walked right on over there to them.

"Happy and Butcher," I said. "We're riding out after that damned Cody. Get over to the office and get our guns ready. Plenty of bullets. Get our horses ready."

"Barjack?" said Happy. "What about your jurisdiction?"

"I done checked on that with ole Peester," I said. "It's legal on account a' the bastards robbed our bank. Now get going."

"Yes, sir," said Happy, and him and Butcher both jumped up and run outta the place.

"Bonnie," I said, "I got to do this."

"I know, sweetie," she said, and she stood up outta her chair and give me a squashing hug. When I got loose and could breathe again, I said, "Have Aubrey pack us up some grub. We could be gone for a while. And a few bottles a' good whiskey."

"Right away, Barjack," she said.

I got my horse and rid over to where Sly lived with my onetime wife and found him home. I ast him to ride along with us, and he agreed. First he had to go to her fancy eating place and tell his snotty wife that he was a-going. Ole Henshaw seed the boys gathering up in front a' my marshaling office, and he come a-running.

"You going after them, Barjack?" he said.

"Damn sure am," I said.

"I want to go along. Oscar Martin was my best friend."

"Well, hurry up and get your ass ready," I said. "You can catch up with us on the road."

"I'll be right behind you," he said, and he run off to get his horse and guns. Sly come riding up then.

"All right," I said. "Let's get our ass going."

We rid off right quicklike, heading out the same way we had gone before. I knowed that we should catch up with Churkee before we come across Cody or any of his three remaining pals. Well, we rid out most a' that day, and we went right past the two trails what them two had tuck to throw us off the trail or else just to get me to split up my posse, and we rid past that place where we had got ambushed. We didn't see no one along the way, and we rid on to the next town. We stopped in front a' their saloon what was a little bitty ole place, not nearly as nice as my Hooch House, and we all went inside and ordered up some whiskey. I had packed some a' my own along in my saddlebags, but I decided to buy me a drink in a saloon instead a' drinking my own stash.

That barkeep was eyeballing my marshal's badge. He shoved my drink up under my nose there at the bar, and then he said, "Town marshal, huh? What town, if you don't mind my asking?"

"Asininity," I said.

"Asininity," he said. "You're Barjack?"

"That's right," I said. "That's my name."

I dranked down my shot a' whiskey and shoved the glass back toward him. He poured another shot. "I've heard about you," he said.

"Good or bad?" I ast him.

"Well, now," he said, "that depends on who it is doing the talking."

"Who was the last one?" I said.

"Feller rode through here not long ago," he said. "Called hisself Cody, I think. He said you was kinda high-handed. Run the town like it was all yours."

"Cody, huh? Is he still around?"

"No. A Indi'n come into town a-looking for him. Cody shot the Indi'n and lit off outta town."

"This Indi'n," I said, "is he kilt?"

"No. He was hurt bad enough, but our doc's got him over in his office. I hear he's mending pretty good."

Well, I turned down my whiskey, and then I said, "Tell me where your doc's office is at."

He tole me, and I headed my ass on outta there. My pards all follered me out. It was across the street and a few doors down. I found it all right, and I barged right in. The doc was a-setting at a desk, and he looked up right surprised when I barged in there.

"My name's Barjack," I said. "I hear you got a friend a' mine in here shot."

"I've got an Indian in the back room," he said.

"How is he?"

"He took a bullet. Pretty bad, but he's getting over it all right. You say he's a friend a' yours?"

"That's what I said. Can I see him?"

The doc nodded his head toward a door on the back wall a' his office, and I went on through it. My pards was all waiting outside on the sidewalk, so it were just me going in there. I stepped through the door, and there was ole Churkee all right. He was setting up in bed, and his chest was all bandaged up.

"Barjack," he said. "What are you doing here?"

"When I found out you run out on me, I follered you," I said.

Chapter Seven

"Are you still after Cody?" Churkee ast me.

"The son of a bitch robbed my bank," I said, "but it don't look to me like as if you're in no shape to ride along just now."

"I don't believe I could even sit a horse right now," he said.

"Well, hell," I said, "then I reckon I'll just have to keep on after him without you. When you come on him, did he have them other three with him?"

"I never saw them."

"I hate to leave you outta this," I said, "but I reckon I just as well get on the road."

"Wait a minute, Barjack," Churkee said. "I think I can save you a lot of riding."

"How's that?"

"If you just go back to Asininity and wait, I believe that Cody will ride right back there."

"Why the hell would he do that?"

"His pride. Didn't you kill one of his men?"

"Well, yeah. That is, the ole Widdamaker done it. What's that got to do with it?"

"Sly got the one that was carrying the money. Right? Well, Cody wants the money, and he wants revenge. He'll go back to Asininity. The only thing is, he won't ride in the way he did before. He'll be sneaking in."

I thunk over what he had said to me for a minute, and then I said, "If I was to get a wagon to haul you in, you want to go back with us?"

"Hell, yes," he said.

Well, I found a wagon all right, but the feller what owned it didn't aim to give it up, so I kinda forced the issue with him. I wound up taking the wagon and giving him a note for payment. I told him he could send the note to ole pettifoggin' Peester for payment. I don't think he believed me none, but he tuck the note anyways, and I tuck the wagon. I waited till I had driv a good distance aways from the son of a bitch before I went and holstered my ole Merwin and Hulbert again. Betwixt me and the other boys, we come up with enough blankets to make ole Miller the Churkee more or less comfortable in the back a' the wagon, and we headed back for Asininity right away. We hadn't got too far down the road, though, afore we all got kinder hungry, so we stopped beside a' the road and built up a fire to cook us up some grub and make some coffee. I pulled a bottle outta my saddlebags and had me a good long snort a' good brown whiskey. I offered some to Miller, thinking that it might help him get his healing did, but he declined it. I thunk that was pretty foolish of him, but I never said nothing about it to him.

We et pretty good for being out on the trail like we was, and we drunk up a good deal a' coffee and most a' my bottle a' whiskey. Course, I had a couple more stashed that I never mentioned, and by and by we loaded up and headed out again. I had Happy and Butcher ride drag and keep a-watching our back end on account a' I weren't sure atall just when that Cody would be headed back for Asininity, and I sure as hell didn't want him to come sneaking up behind us and give us a hell of a surprise like that. I looked over my shoulder ever' now and than anyhow. But we never seed nothing of them coming. We rid on like that till it come dark, and then we stopped for the night and made us a camp. We built another fire and laid us out some beds for the night.

Butcher hadn't never slept out from under no roof before, and he was some nervous about maybe a snake would come crawling up on him, so I final had him lay out his bed on the wagon seat and sleep up there. That helped him some, and I reckon he final got some sleep in spite a' not having a roof over his head. I made Happy stay awake and watch for a few hours, and then ole Sly tuck his place. After Sly had did his spell, I tuck a turn at it. Nothing ever come up on us, though.

When morning come, we had us some breakfast, and then we headed on into Asininity, what we made it in to by midafternoon. I had the boys drop Miller off at ole Doc's, and then the rest of us, all except Sly a' course, what went home to his wife, all the rest of us went to the Hooch House and got at my table and got us some drinks delivered over by ole Aubrey. Bonnie was sure as hell happy to see me. I could tell by the way she damn near squoze me to death right there in front a' the whole damn world. You know, it sure is a great comfort in this wild and wicked world to have yourself someone what loves you like that. It makes life worth living. It makes it more easier to face the dangers and the devilments what you just naturally has to face from day to day.

"Goddamn it, Bonnie," I said, "turn a-loose a' me. You're a-wrinkling my suit."

We set down side by side, and she helt on to my arm. "Did you miss me, honey?" she said.

"Why, sure, I missed you, sweet nipples," I said, giving one a' her great big boobs a loving squeeze.

"Not here," she said, gouging a elbow into my side and damn near breaking a couple a' my ribs.

"Ow," I yelped, and I scooted my chair a little ways away from her. Then I picked up my whiskey glass and tuck a good gulp out of it.

"Barjack?" said Happy.

"Whut?"

"Do you think that Cody feller will come back to Asininity?"

"Miller knows him better'n I do," I said. "Now, what the hell did Miller say about that?"

"Well," Happy said, "I think that Miller said he'd be coming back on account a' he wanted his revenge on you and on account a' he still wants that money what Sly got back from them."

"I ain't got nothing to add to that," I said.

"Well," Happy said, "when do you think he'll be here?"

"I can't say nothing about that neither," I said. "Hell, he might could come walking in here right now for all I know, or it might be next week or next month. How the hell would I know?"

"I guess you wouldn't," he kinda mumbled, and picked up his drink and had a sip.

"Barjack," Butcher said, "when he does get here,

what're we going to do? I mean, do we just sit here and wait till we see him walk through that door?"

"No, Butcher," I said, getting kindly aggravated at the both of them, "I want you and Happy to get your rifles and go outside and climb up on a roof and watch for them."

"Yes, sir," he said. "Uh, right now?"

"Right now," I said. "One of you on one side a' the street and t'other'n on t'other side. Drink up and get on outta here."

They both dranked up their drinks and headed for the door, and I breathed me a huge ass sigh a' relief when they was gone. And I was giving my thanks that neither one a' the bastards had ast me which roof to crawl up on.

Bonnie scooched her chair over close to me again and tuck hold a' my arm right tight. "Barjack," she said, "that man's coming back after you now, ain't he?"

"Well, now, honey butt," I said, "that there is just speculation is all. I don't rightly know if he's a-coming back or not. If he's a damn fool, he might."

"I don't want nothing to happen to you," she said, and I glanced over at her round face, and the look in her eyes damn near made me cry, but I looked away again right quick, and I tuck me another drink real fast too. "Let's go upstairs," she said. I turned my glass back and drained it dry and shoved my chair back and stood up.

"Well, come on, sweetness," I said, and she clung on to my arm as we walked across the room and on up the stairs. I noticed as we made our way over there that Dingle was a-scribbling in his notebook.

When we final got to the top a' the stairs, I paused and looked back over the big room down below me. I guess I was taking one last look for that god-damned Cody, but I never seed no sign of him, nor of no strangers neither. I walked on down the hall-way with Bonnie, and we turned into our room.

Pretty damn soon, we was bouncing around so much on that damn bed and making so goddamn much noise that I was almost sure for certain that ever'one downstairs underneath us in that big noisy saloon could hear us all right. Final we both of us wore our ass out and we quit. For a while we just lay there side by side and still nekkid as jay-birds and petted around on each other and giggled like silly kids.

It were still early in the evening, and I final got up and went to pulling on my clothes. Bonnie weren't far behind me in that. Whenever I started in to strap my six-gun around my waist, Bonnie said, "Barjack, get me one a' them."

"One a' what, Bonnie?" I said.

"A gun belt and a six-gun," she said.

I shoulda knowed better than to say what I said next, but I usual learn the hard way. So I said, "I don't think I got a belt long enough to go around you, darling."

She slugged me hard on my shoulder and grabbed a holt a' my gun belt, jerking it away from me. Then she put it around her own waist, but she couldn't get the belt to come together in front of her.

"I told you," I said.

She slung my Merwin and Hulbert in its holster back at me by the end a' the belt, and it hit me in the gut right hard, damn near knocking the wind outta me. I made a whoofing sound as I grabbed the gun. Then I started again to strapping it on.

"Well, get me one," she said. "I don't care how or where. I don't give a damn if you have to skin ole Peester. Just get me one, and I mean it."

"I'll check in the office in the morning," I said.

"You do it now, goddamn it," she said.

"I'll go over there right now," I said.

"You do that, and you get your ass back over here right fast too."

"Yes. I will."

I went out the door, and she yelled after me, "And when you come back, have that goddamned rig for me."

"I will," I yelled back over my shoulder. I was already on the stairs.

When I was about halfway down the stairs I called out to Aubrey for a drink. He poured it, and I picked it up from him as I was hurrying on through the place. I went out the batwing doors and onto the sidewalk, and I hurried on down to my marshaling office. First thing I done was I set down behind my desk and tuck myself a good long drink. Then I put the glass down, and I got up and went over to the gun cabinet, and I went through all the rigs what I had stored up in there, but I never found one with a belt long enough. I found a couple that would go around my middle but just barely, so I knowed that none of them would reach around Bonnie.

Then I final got me the idee to pull out two a' them belts and buckle them together to make one real long one. I done that, but the goddamn thing was so damn long that I knowed Bonnie would knock me on my ass if I tuck it to her thattaway. I had to really rack my stupid brain then. Final, I slipped the longass belt through the loop on a holster, and I slipped a .38 caliber Merwin and Hulbert pocket pistol into the holster. I knowed that it wouldn't kick as much as a .45. Then I kinder rolled up the belt and struck my ass back toward the Hooch House.

Soon as I stepped back through the doors I seed ole Bonnie a-setting at my table. Dingle was there too. He was still a-scribbling. There wasn't no one else at the table. I figgered my two brilliant depitties was setting on rooftops somewheres out there. I walked on over to the table, calling for a drink as I did, and by the time I had set down, Aubrey was setting my drink in front a' me. I unrolled that there long belt and reached over and hung it over Bonnie's head, and I draped the belt right betwixt her big titties and fixed it so that there five-shooter was a-hanging at her waist on the left side so that she could grab it with her right hand. One a' them two belts had bullet holders on it, and it was full up with extry shells. Bonnie looked just thrilled at her new rig, so I figgered I had did all right after all.

"That there shooter's loaded, babe," I said. "It's a Merwin and Hulbert self-extracting revolver, just like mine, only it's a mite smaller. For a lady, or for a gentleman's coat pocket." She pulled the shooter outta the holster, and she held it out and studied it.

"It only holds five bullets," I said, "on account a' it's a littler gun, but you got plenty a' extries on that there belt."

She went to fondling the extry bullets on the belt with her left hand, and then she throwed her right arm around me. The gun was still in her right hand. "Oh, Barjack," she said, "I love it. It's just right. Is there anyone in here what needs to get shot?"

"Don't go crazy with it now," I said.

"I'm just kidding you," she said.

Final she set back and slipped that shooter back into the holster where it had ought to be.

"Now, Barjack," she said, "if that no-good bastard dares to come back to Asininity a-looking to hurt my man, I'll be waiting for him, and I'll be ready."

Now, goddamn it, I knowed that she meant it. I knowed that she would be ready for him too.

Chapter Eight

Well, things got pretty quiet around Asininity for the next several days, and I begin to wonder, should I have tuck out another posse after that goddamned Cody bastard. But then I figgered that I had done let it go for too damn long. If he was going to hit us again, it seemed to me that he woulda done did it, and if he didn't have no intention a' hitting us again, he was most likely long gone, to California or some damn place.

Well, ole Miller the Churkee was up and around final, although he was moving some slow and careful. I was glad to have him back hanging around the Hooch House again. We was all in there one day about midafternoon, me and Miller and Dingle and Butcher and Happy and Bonnie, all just a-setting around my own private table and drinking and talking bullshit, when ole Knothead Simpson yelled out from the front door, "Stage is coming in." Well, with all the lack of excitement around the place, we all got up and walked outside to see who or what might be a-coming into town. Sly come outta his wife's place across the street, and he seed me and give me a wave. I hollered a howdy at him.

The stage come to a rolling stop in front a' the

depot, and folks commenced to bailing out. There was a young cowpoke and then a drummer and then a young gal what was dressed in men's clothes and wearing a six-gun strapped around her waist. She come off and stood in the street and kindly looked around like she was a-hunting something or somebody. I remember that I thunk that she coulda been a real beauty if she had a-dressed herself up proper, but I wasn't thinking no other kinda thoughts about her. I had let my ass get hooked up to my ex-wife on account a' her looks, and I didn't have no intention a' letting nothing like that happen again. I was plenty happy and content with my sweet Bonnie, and I was tuck plenty good care of too.

Still, I was town marshal, and that little gal looked kinda lost to me, so I walked over to her, and I kinda tipped my hat and smiled at her. "Excuse me, ma'am," I said, "I'm Barjack. Town marshal here. I wonder if I could be of any assistance to you."

"Thank you. No," she said.

"Well," I said, not giving up so easy, "was you a-looking for someone to meet you here?"

"No. I don't know anyone here."

Just then a blanket roll landed right beside her what the lunk-headed driver had throwed down, and she bent over to pick it up.

"Is that your whole entire luggage?" I ast her.

"I travel light," she said.

"Well, if you need a place to stay, we got some rooms right inside here in the Hooch House. They ain't fancy, but they're clean enough and reasonable priced."

"Thank you," she said. "Who do I see?"

I looked over my shoulder at Bonnie standing there on the sidewalk, and I called out to her, "Bonnie. This here gal wants a room."

"Come on, honey," Bonnie said. "I'll set you up."

The gal walked over to the walkway to join Bonnie, and then the two of them went inside together. Me and the boys all went back to my table inside.

"Barjack," said Happy, "who is she?"

"Who?" I said, even though I knowed perfect well who the hell he was talking about.

"That gal from the stage," he said. "You was talking to her."

"Oh," I said, "that gal."

"Yeah," said Happy. "Well?"

"Well, whut?"

"Who is she?"

"She never said," I answered him.

"You didn't ask her?"

"Nope."

"That ain't like you, Barjack."

"It ain't?"

"No, it ain't. You most always finds out who a stranger is whenever he comes to town."

"Oh, well, she ain't a he."

"Is that how come you never ast her who she is?"

"No, hell, I just didn't do it. That's all."

Happy, he kindly shuck his head and ducked it a little and muttered, "That ain't like you."

I never bothered to answer him that time. I just tuck me another drink a' my whiskey, and then my glass was emptied, and so I lifted it up high and kindly wiggled it around a bit to get Aubrey's attention. He come quick to refill it.

Bonnie had tuck the gal upstairs to show her the

room, and just then they come back down the stairs. Bonnie was still a-wearing her new Merwin and Hulbert .38 hanging around her neck and shoulder. She brung that gal right over to my table and they both set down. Bonnie waved at ole Aubrey, and he come over to take care a' them.

Bonnie looked at the gal. "I think you done met Barjack," she said.

"I did."

"Well, these others is Mr. Dingle. He's a book writer, and he's writ some books about my Barjack. And these two is Barjack's depitties. Happy Bonapart and Butcher Doyle. Butcher come out here from New York City. And final, this here is Mr. Mose Miller. He's a real Churkee Indian."

They all howdied her real politelike, and then Bonnie said, "Fellows, this here is Miss Pistol Polly McGuire."

"Pistol?" I said.

"Folks what knows me," she said, "started into calling me that on account a' I'm pretty handy with this here." She hauled out a .45-caliber Smith & Wesson revolver and went to spinning it around her finger. Then she put it up again.

"Uh, Barjack," said Happy, "don't our law about toting guns in town apply to womenfolks as well as to men?"

"Never mind about that, Happy," I said. "Well, Miss Pistol Polly, how would you like to ride outta town with us to do a little shooting? Target practice, I should say."

"I'd like that fine," she said. "I could use a little shooting practice all right." Then she drunk down her glass a' whiskey.

"Can I go too, Barjack?" Bonnie said.

"Sure you can, sweet ass," I said.

"Right now? Are we going now?"

"Hell, yes," I said. "Happy, have Aubrey fill up a big sack with empty bottles and bring it along. Dingle, you coming with us?"

"Yes," he said.

"All right. Go down to the stable then and get us all a horse and bring them down here."

Happy and Dingle both got up and left to do what I told them to do. Then I said, "Butcher, run down to my marshaling office and get a bunch a' bullets. Forty-fives and thirty-eights, and fetch them back down here."

"Yes, sir," said ole Butcher, and he jumped up and run.

Well, sir, there ain't much reason for me to go on in no amount a' detail about our shooting practice. We went to where we had all went before, all except for Polly Pistol, that is, and we all us shot up a bunch a' shells. We had picked up ole Sly along the way too. Ole Dingle done a little bit better than what he done before, and Butcher and Happy done all right too. I didn't exact embarrass myself neither. But what damn sure surprised the hell outta me was the damn fine shooting a' that Polly Pistol. Hell, she outshot all of us excepting ole Sly, and for a while there I thunk she was a-going to beat him. By God, if I was a-fixing to have a big ole shoot-out with a bunch a owl hoots, I'd a sure wanted her standing on my side. She could pull and shoot faster'n a rattlesnake strikes. I sure did admire her style.

Oh yeah, I damn near forgot to say anything

about my sweet tits, ole Bonnie Boodle. She done about as well as Butcher and Happy. I had almost forgot that Bonnie could handle a six-gun, or in this case, a five-shooter. I remember thinking whilst we was all out there a-shooting that we made a pretty damn good little army, we did.

We was all a-riding horseback back into town, and I brung myself up alongside Miss Polly Pistol.

"Miss Polly," I said, "you really done yourself proud out there today. If you don't mind me saying it, you're a damn good shooter."

"Thank you, Marshal," she said.

"How come you to get so good at it?"

"My daddy taught me to shoot when I was ten years old," she said. "He told me, you never know when you might need it. I kept up my practice all these years."

Well, a' course, I never knowed how old she was, and I admit that I did wonder just how many years she was talking about. I guessed, though, that she sure as hell weren't yet thirty. Anyhow, she'd had a-plenty a' practice, and that there's for sure and certain.

"Could I ask you," I said, "what the hell brought you to Ashitniy of all damn places?"

"Sure," she said. "You got a right to know, being town marshal and all. I'm hunting a man I mean to kill."

"Oh?" I said, kinda stupidlike. But I thunk about what it was she said, and I could sure see her doing it. I hadn't knowed many men who could beat her in a gunfight. Course, shooting bottles off a log and shooting a live man what is shooting back at you is two whole and entire different things. Still, if it come to it, I woulda bet on Polly, and you can believe that.

"You most likely want to know a little more about it," Polly said.

"Well, I—"

"I'll tell you. I come from down around Baxter Springs, Kansas."

"I been there," I said.

"Well, a man come through a few months ago, and he went to courting me. I admit I fell for him. I fell hard. He was a pretty good-looking fellow, and he was a real gentleman too. Finally, he proposed marriage to me, and I accepted. We set a date, but before it come up, he went and seduced my baby sister. He left her pregnant. When she told me about it, he had done left town, so I packed up and took off after his ass."

"Well," I said, clearing my throat kind a nervous-like, "I reckon I can't blame you for that. You think he come through Asininity, do you?"

"I'm pretty damn sure about it," she said.

"What's the son of a bitch's name?" I said. "Maybe I heared of him."

"The son of a bitch is named Hiram Cody," she said. "He pronounces it like harm, and that's what most folks call him. Well, I tell you, I mean to harm him all right. I mean to harm him right into his grave."

"Well, Miss Polly," I said, "that is a hell of a thing. He has sure as hell been through Asininity. He come through with a handful a' tough guys and they robbed our bank. I went after them with a posse,

most of which is right here with us, and one a' the
gang got hisself kilt, and we recovered the money,
but we never did catch up with that goddamned
Harm fellow."

"Which way was he headed?" she said.

"Last I knowed," I said, "he was moving south,
but that ain't all."

"I'm listening," she said.

"There's someone else on his trail."

"Who?"

"The Churkee name a' Mose Miller. He was at my
Hooch House earlier. He's got his reasons too, but
he was with my posse, and he got hisself shot up
some. That's why he didn't come shooting, he's still
recooper—whatever you call it—getting better."

"I'd like to talk to him," she said.

"I reckon we can deal with that," I said. "I was
going to go after that damn Harm again, but someone said he would most likely be coming back to
Asininity, so I decided to take a chance that he
would do that."

"Why would he come back?" she ast me.

"To get the money what we tuck back from him,"
I said, "and maybe to get hisself a little revenge, you
know."

"Yeah," she said, kinda slow, like she was a-thinking about it. "He might just do that."

"And he might have three or four men with him
whenever he does," I said.

"He can have a goddamned army," Polly said.
"I'll still get his ass."

And I believed she would too. Right about then,
ole Bonnie got suspicious about me riding along

and talking with Polly for so long, and she rid up and kinda squeezed in betwixt us, so we cut out our talking.

"Cute ass," I said, "you done pretty good out there today. I reckon I ain't askeered a' letting you tote that there little Merwin and Hulbert atall."

"Thanks, Barjack," she said. "Course, I ain't near as good as Miss Polly here."

"I think you can take care a' yourself all right," I told her.

"I'm more interested in taking keer a' you," she said, "in case that damn Cody comes back to Asininity a-looking for you."

"Oh yeah," I said, "Miss Polly here is after that son of a bitch too."

"What?" Bonnie said. "What for?"

I let Polly tell her whole tale all over again, this time for the benefit of ole Bonnie, and then Bonnie was real hot after his ass.

"If you don't get the son of a bitch," she said to Polly, "I'll get him for you."

I was thinking that it was kinda nice to have two gunslinging females a-watching out for me. When we had made it back into town, I had Happy take Miss Polly up to see the Churkee, and made Dingle get the horses back to the stable. Then I led the way back into the Hooch House to my private table. Ole Aubrey seed us come in and served drinks all around right away. Even Sly set down with us to have one.

Chapter Nine

Well, I guess I had to be put to bed again that night. I don't really recall nothing atall about it. The last thing I remember was setting there feeling a bit woozy and having another drink a' my good whiskey, and then I woked up in my own bed with ole Bonnie a-snoring away right next to me. I eased my ass outta that bed real careful-like and got myself dressed and went downstairs a-hunting a drink and some breakfast. I was real pleasant surprised to find damn near the whole gang already there a-setting at my own private table.

"Well, goddamn," I said, "who the hell invited all a' you here this morning?"

Butcher and Happy stood up right quick, and ole Happy, he said, "I'm sorry, Barjack. We can go somewhere else."

"Oh, set your ass back down," I said. "Can't you never tell when it is you're a-being joshed around?"

They both set back down, and right about then, ole Aubrey called out to me from over behind the bar. "Coffee and whiskey, Barjack?" he said.

"Yeah, Aubrey," I said. "As fast as ever you can."

He was purty fast too, and the first thing I done

was I tuck myself a slug a' that whiskey. Then I sipped some coffee. Then I looked up at Aubrey, still standing right there, and I said, "Bring me my breakfast too." He said, "Yes, sir," and he hustled off to get it did.

About then that Miss Polly come in, and she seed us and come right on over to set down with us. She ordered a breakfast and some coffee, and she how-died ever'one around the table. They all howdied her right back.

"Well, hell," I said, "has anyone kilt anyone while I was a-sleeping?"

"No, sir," said Happy. "It was a right quiet night."

"That's right, Marshal," Butcher said. "I didn't hear nothing but one ole barking pup."

"Nobody even shot the pup," said Dingle, looking up for just a bit from his scribbling.

"I thought about going out to find it and shoot it myself," Polly said.

Just then Bonnie come a-bouncing down the stairs, her tits looking like two big old water skins on the deck of a schooner at sea during a hellacious gale. She come right over to me and give me a big wet, slobbery kiss, and then she give loud cheerful greetings to ever'one around the table. She was a-wearing that gun hanging around her neck too. Final she set down by my side.

Well, I et my food and dranked several cups a' coffee and the rest a' the glass a' whiskey, and then I said, "Say, has anyone a' you bastards seed that old Churkee late?"

No one had, so I went on, "I think I'll run over and check on him. See how he's doing."

So I left them all a-setting at my table and went

outside and on over to Doc's place. When I went in there, there weren't no sign a' Doc, so I just peeked into the back room. There weren't no sign a' Churkee in there neither. "Well, goddamn me," I said. I opened ever' other door in the place, but I never found no sign a' Doc or Miller, so I headed back for the Hooch House a-scratching my head. As I was walking along I spied ole Doc coming outta Lillian's fancy eating establishment and I give him a loud yell. He answered me and we met up in the middle a the street.

"What can I do for you, Marshal?" he ast me.

"I just come outta your office," I said, "and I couldn't find no Churkee. Where the hell is he?"

"He got hisself up early this morning and left out," Doc said. "I tried to stop him, but he wouldn't listen to me. I told him it was too soon, but he said he had stuff to take keer of."

"Goddamn," I said.

"Wasn't nothing I could do about it."

I left Doc and walked on to the stable, where I found out that Miller had got his horse, saddled it up, and rid outta town headed south. He was packing his six-guns and a Winchester. I cussed again and went on back to the Hooch House. I was still a-cussing whenever I set back down by Bonnie, and a' course, she wanted to know how come.

"What the hell's wrong with you, Barjack?" she said.

"Oh, that damned Churkee," I said.

"What about him?"

"He went and got hisself outta bed and got his guns and his horse and tuck off, heading south," I said.

"He's gone after that Cody," said Happy. "I'll betcha."

"Hell, yes, that's what he's did," I said. "What else?"

"Well, are we going after him, Barjack?" said Butcher.

"No, we ain't," I said. "He never ast me. And there ain't no telling where that son of a bitch Cody is at by this time. What if we was to catch up to Miller and find out that he's done kilt Cody? Then what sense would it make that we had went after him? Tell me that."

"Well," said Happy, "what if we was to find out that Cody had killed Miller?"

"It would be outside a' my jurisdiction," I said, "and there wouldn't be nothing we could do about it. But most likely, we would catch up with Miller and find out that he hadn't come across Cody atall, and we still wouldn't have no idee how far south the son of a bitch had got to. We ain't going nowhere, and I don't want to hear no more about it."

"Okay, Barjack," Happy said.

"Just shut up about it," I said.

"All right," said Happy.

Polly, what was a-setting there too, downed her drink and said, "Well, I'd go after him, but I don't want Miller gunning him. I want to catch up to him by my lonesome."

"Well, hell," I said, "Miller's apt to get him first."

"He might," she said, "but you told me a while back that Harm's liable to come back here. I might as well hang around for a spell and see."

"Do whatever it is you want to do," I told her. "I don't give a shit."

"I aim to," she said.

"That goddamned stupid Churkee is apt to get hisself kilt," I said.

"I thought you didn't want to talk about it no more," said Happy.

"I don't, so just shut up about it."

"Yes, sir."

Happy was just about to piss me off with his goddamn silliness. I guess Bonnie could see it, on account a' she of a sudden invited me to go upstairs with her. I finished off my drink and allowed her to take me along. We was upstairs a-bouncing around for a spell, and we wound up by just a-laying there on the bed together, still nekkid as a couple of damn jaybirds.

"What's wrong, Barjack?" she said.

"Ain't nothing wrong," I said. "What made you ask me such a question anyhow?"

"You're sullen," she said. "Kinda almost poutinglike."

"Well, there ain't nothing wrong, and that's that."

"Now, looky here," she said. "I can tell when you got something on your mind. You just—"

"I don't want to hear no more about it," I snapped back at her.

"All right," she said, and she got up and started in to getting dressed again. I watched her a-wiggling her fat ass into her underthings and then into her dress. It made me think about someone a-trying to stuff a bunch a' live quail into a sack. When I got tired a' watching, I got up to pull on my clothes. In a few more minutes we was back down to my table. The ole Widdamaker had come in and set down. He stood up and doffed his hat to ole Bonnie and made her giggle like a silly little girl.

"Howdy, Sly," I said.

Aubrey brung me and Bonnie our drinks, and Bonnie, on account a' Sly was there, I think, thanked Aubrey real kindlylike. I was already drinking outta mine.

"Hey," said Happy, "it's Miller."

"What the hell?" I said. "I told you I don't wanta hear no more about—"

"No, Barjack," Happy said. "He's here."

I twisted around to look, and sure enough, here come the Churkee walking straight over to my table. Ever'one howdied him, and he pulled out a chair and set his ass down.

"I had just about figgered you was dead," I said.

"No," he said, "but I found him."

"Where?" said Polly.

"I came across his camp on the road," Miller said.

"And you never kilt him?" I said.

"He has twelve men with him," said Miller. "I didn't think the odds were in my favor."

"Twelve?" said Butcher.

"They're coming back here," Miller said.

"How do you know that?" I ast him.

"I managed to sneak up close to the camp and listen in on their conversation. They're planning to hit Asininity tomorrow evening just before the bank closes. They mean to rob the bank and kill you, Barjack. Cody thinks they killed me already. Then they plan to burn the town down. The whole place, starting with the Hooch House."

"They'll play hell trying," said Bonnie, grabbing on to her six-shooter with her right hand. She never pulled it out, though.

"You heared all that for sure?" I ast him.

"I did," he said. "For sure."

"Tomorrow night?" I said.

"Yes, sir," he said. "Tomorrow night."

I looked over and seen ole Dingle a-scribbling away. "We'll be ready for them," I said. I stood up.

"Where you going, Barjack?" said Bonnie.

"I'm a-going down to my marshaling office to think this over. I got to make some plans." I thunk a bit before I headed on out, and then I said, "Happy, come on along with me." He jumped up to foller me along.

"Yes, sir," he said.

The first thing I done whenever we was in my marshaling office was to take out my bottle what was stashed in a desk drawer along with a couple a' glasses and pour us each a drink. Then I tuck a good long slug outta mine. "Happy," I said, "we got to get our ass braced for them bastards. They think that with thirteen of them all told they're just going to ride in here and wipe us out. Well, it ain't a-going to happen like that."

"So what will we do, Barjack?"

"I aim to put you and Butcher up on the roofs of our two southern-most buildings. You on one side and Butcher on t'other, each one a' you with a rifle and a extry box a' shells. Whatever one a' you sees them a-coming first, stand up and wave your hat three times over your head. That'll signal the rest of us. I'll put Dingle and Miller inside of a couple a' buildings a little farther down. They'll have rifles too. Polly too if she wants to. Me and Sly will meet them out in the middle a' the street."

"That's still seven to thirteen," he said.

"Hell, I know it. I figure each one of us can pick off at least two of them."

"Yeah. I reckon so."

"All right then," I said. "We'll do it thattaway. We'll have to tell the others right away. And we'll get set up tomorrer afternoon to be sure we're ready for them whenever they ride in."

"We'll give the bastards a hell of a surprise, won't we, Barjack?"

"We sure as hell will, Happy. That's the general idee."

I told Happy to stand up and wave his hat as soon as he seed them coming, and then we walked back down to the Hooch House. We told Butcher and Dingle and Miller and Polly and Bonnie all about our plan, and they each one agreed with it. Ole Bonnie, she insisted that she take part in the defense of Asininity, so I tole her that I'd put her in a storefront too.

"With a rifle," she said.

"With a goddamned rifle and a extry box a' shells," I said.

So that was ever'one 'cept old Sly, and I tole them that I had to go locate him and tell him all about it. I finished a drink and went out to look for him. He weren't in Lillian's, that's his wife and my ex-wife's fancy eating place, and she tole me that he must be at home with the brat. I didn't really want to go to that goddamned house what used to be mine, nor I didn't want to see the little brat what used to be mine, but I sure as hell did need to see the Widda-maker, so I headed on over in that direction.

Whenever I got over there, I never noticed it at first, but the damn little brat was up in a bois d'arc tree in front a' the house. As I walked on toward the front door, the little shit throwed a goddamned big horse apple at me, and it smacked me right atop a' the head. It's a damn good thing I had my hat on. As it was, it raised a lump, and it knocked me off a' my feet. I landed facedown in the grass, and I heared him a-snickering up there. Soon as I was able, I got back up on my feet and I located the little shit, and I shuck my fist at him.

"You little fucker," I yelled. "You get your ass down here, and I'll by God skin it for you."

I made so damn much noise that it brung old Sly out the front door. "Barjack?" he said. I turned around to see him, and he said, "What's wrong?"

"Aw, nothing," I said. "I come to see you about a little problem."

"Well, come on over and sit down," he said. He had a couple a' chairs in front a' the house, and I walked over there and set in one. He set in the other'n. "What's on your mind?" he said.

I tole him how Churkee had struck out on his own and had come across that damn Cody and twelve other men camped. He sneaked up on them and listened to them plotting how they was going to hit Asininity just before the bank closing tomor-rer, and how they meant to kill me and then burn down the whole damn town. I give him my plan of action.

"Why do you want us to meet them in the street?" he said.

"I ain't real sure," I said. "I guess it's my god-damned sense a' fair play. Give them a chance to give up and go to jail. If you got a better idee, I'm a-listening."

"No," he said. "I'll meet them with you."

"Side by side," I said.

Chapter Ten

Well, it come about bank closing time, and I sent the boys out to take up their positions. Dingle and Polly was told to watch the rooftops, and if Butcher or Happy was to see that Cody and his bunch a-headed into town, whichever one of them seed them was supposed to stand up and wave his hat. Then the rest of us would know and we'd all get ready for the bastards. Me and Sly was setting in my marshaling office and waiting. I had me a glass a' whiskey, but the Widdamaker, he turned it down. He never done no drinking before killing. Afterward, sometimes he'd have a drink or two, but never before. Of a sudden, my front door bursted open and ole Polly come a-crashing in.

"They're coming, Barjack," she said. "At least, I think they're coming."

"What the hell do you mean by that?" I said. "Are they coming or ain't they?"

"Well," she said, "Happy stood up down there on his roof, and he took off his hat and started in to waving it. He waved it over his head two and a half times. Then he sat back down."

"Two and a half times?" I said. "Maybe he just waved a little short that last time."

"No," she said. "He definitely quit halfway through the wave."

"So he waved—"

"Two and a half times."

"Goddamn," I said. "Come on, Sly."

The three of us run out the front door a' the office. Polly went back to her store winder, and me and ole Sly went a-walking toward the end a' town in the direction they'd be a-coming from. When we got down close, I yelled up toward the rooftop where I had posted Happy.

"Happy," I yelled out. "Happy, you silly son of a bitch."

Happy popped up and called back down to me, "Yeah, Barjack?"

"Did you wave two and a half times at us?"

"Yes, sir," he said. "I sure did."

"Well, now, just what the hell does two and a half waves mean, if you don't mind explaining that to me?"

"No," he said. "I don't mind."

"All right then, goddamn it, I'm a-waiting."

"Well, Barjack, they're a-coming all right, but they's only six of them."

"Six?" I said, and I looked at Sly. "What do you reckon that means?"

"I don't know, Barjack," Sly said. "It could be most anything, Maybe he figures he only needs six for the job, or maybe the rest are coming in a few minutes later, or maybe they circled around and will be hitting us from another direction. I can't read Cody's mind. I don't know him."

"Well, hell, are you ready for them?" I ast him, and I was kindly shaking, I don't mind telling you.

"I'm ready," he said.

"Well, uh, let's get over on the sidewalk," I said. "We make too good a target out here like this."

"Okay," he said, and the two of us walked over to stand on the walk. That put us in the shadow too, and I felt a little bit better about it. It weren't but a few seconds later whenever I heared the sound a their horses a-coming, and then real quick after that I seed them. They come a-riding on in, and I fired a shot up into the air and yelled out.

"Hold up there," I called out to them.

They was startled. Their horses commenced to jumping around some on them. "What the hell?" one of them said. Then me and Sly, we walked out into the street with our six-guns in our hands.

"All right, boys," I said, "toss down your guns. I'm a-taking you to jail."

One a' them hauled out his six-gun, and Sly shot him off a' his horse. Then the other five all reached for theirs. I nicked one in the shoulder, and then a rifle shot from off one a' the roofs knocked him plumb out a' the saddle. The other four jumped off a' their horses and tuck out a-running for cover. A couple of them was shooting as they run. I fell down on my face. I don't know what Sly done. What I do know is that of a sudden it sounded like a small war broke out in Asininity. I raised my head up real slowlike so as not to draw no undue attention to the fact that I was alive and went to rolling my eyeballs around to see what I could see.

There was a outlaw crouched down behind a water trough not far from me, but he was paying attention to the storefronts and the rooftops, what made a certain amount a' sense. The gunshots was still a-popping all around. I seed another one what had run for the corner a' the first building and was standing there a-peering around the corner. He was shooting at Butcher on a rooftop across the street from where he was at. I ain't atall sure where the other'ns was at. It come to me that I could hit the feller around the corner. I had a good shot at him, and he weren't paying me no mind atall. He musta thunk I was already done for. I slipped my Merwin and Hulbert out real slow and worked it up to where I could point it at him. I waited for him to come out from behind the corner just a little bit to shoot at Butcher, and then I pulled the trigger. I seed where the bullet tore through his damned neck, and his head kinda bobbed around a bit. His legs went all rubbery, and he collapsed. So they was still three more as far as I could tell.

Since I had fired a shot, I figgered that I had give my ass away, and I got up on my feet as fast as ever I could and run for cover. A couple a bullets nicked at my heels as I run and when I went up on the sidewalk, one hit one a' the uprights what was holding up the overhanging roof just as I run past it. I ducked into a doorway what was kindly set in and give me some cover. Then I looked around. I seed that feller behind the horse trough. He was still there and still a-shooting. I wondered where the other two was a-hiding. The best thing I could think of to say about the whole situation was that they wasn't in the bank.

So I hauled out my ole shooter and commenced to blasting away at that tank and the feller what was hiding behind it. I punched about four holes in that trough before I final drilled the son of a bitch. Whenever I hit him, he kindly rose up and then pitched forward, dropping his top half into the trough but hanging over the edge. He never moved after that, so I figgered that if my bullet hadn't a-kilt him, then he drowned hisself in that horse trough. Either way he was dead as hell. There was still two of them left alive and shooting.

It still sounded like a small war a-going on. The six horses them outlaws had rid into town was still a-milling around loose in the street. A couple of them had been wounded in all the shooting, but four of them was okay far as I could tell. Two a' them had run down to the far end a' the street where they was safe enough, but the remaining two was dancing and a-prancing right out in the middle a' the war. I heared a voice then. "Mac," it said, "let's make for the horses and get the hell outta here." Then one a' them bastards bursted out a' hiding, and by God, he was hiding in the doorway right next to where I was hiding. He run straight for the nearest horse. He was just about to swing up into the saddle whenever I shot him in his goddamn leg. He yowled out loud like hell and fell down in the street. The horse nickered and run off.

Then the one what was called Mac run out into the street from somewhere on the other side a' the street, and he was shooting at me. I guess he had saw me whenever I shot his pardner. I ducked back into that doorway and pressed myself back hard against the wall. Then I heared a shot and seed him jerk and twitch and final flop down in the dirt, where he kicked around a bit before he final lay still and looked dead. And then I seed ole Bonnie step out the door a' the place where I had hid her away. She had a Henry rifle in her hands, and she stood on the sidewalk a-looking at the son of a bitch she had shot.

"That's what you get for threatening to burn down my Hooch House and kill my Barjack," she said, and then all of us come outta hiding.

"Well, Barjack," said Sly, walking up to me, "that should teach them not to come riding into your town to make trouble."

"It had ought to teach them all right," I said, "but that damn Cody ain't here and he's still out there somewhere with six more a' the sons a' bitches."

"I know where they're camped," Miller said. "We could ride out and get them before they know what's happened."

Bonnie come running to me and throwed her arms around me and like to knocked me over. I woulda fell down for sure if she hadn't a-been hanging on to me so hard. "Barjack," she said, "are you all right?"

"The bastards never touched me," I said.

"Barjack," Happy yelled out from his rooftop, "can me and Butcher come down now?"

"Come on down, you two," I hollered back at them. Then I looked around, and ever'one was gathered around me. I waited a minute or two for Happy and Butcher to show up. That ole boy I had shot in the leg was a-moaning and groaning, and Sly walked over to him and got his shooter away from him and jerked him up to his feet. "Butcher," I said, "take that son of a bitch over to the jailhouse and lock him up. Happy, go fetch Doc over to take care a' his shot leg. But you don't need to hurry none."

"He might could bleed to death, Barjack," Happy said.

"Don't worry none about that," I said. "When you've did that, go to the stable and get all our horses, and get horses for anyone else who wants to ride along with us."

"Yes, sir," he said, and he started out.

"We going out after the rest of them?" Sly ast me.

"Miller had a pretty good idee," I said.

"They'll hear us coming," said Butcher.

"They'll think it's this bunch coming back to camp," said Miller. "They won't know better till it's too late."

"That's right," I said. "It's the best chance we'll have. Catch them off guard."

Ole Bonnie and Pistol Polly and Dingle the Scribbler all hurried off toward the stable, so whilst the rest of us was standing around a waiting for them and for Happy to get back with the horses, I said to Sly, "Let's stroll on over to my office and have a drink before we get gathered up and head out."

"Barjack," he said, "I'd better go tell Lillian what we're doing. She'll be wondering about me."

"Well, hell, all right," I said, "but we'll be heading out right quick."

"I'll be with you," he said. "Don't worry."

I walked on over to my marshaling office and went inside. Butcher was just locking the cell door on that damned owl hoot. "Got him locked up, Marshal," he said.

"Good."

"I'm bleeding to death in here," the bastard whined.

"See if you can't get it did before the doc gets here," I said. "Save us all a lot of trouble."

"You son of a bitch," he snarled.

I pulled the bottle and a glass outta my desk drawer and poured myself a snort. It burned real good going down, so I poured another'n. I looked up at ole Butcher a-standing there. "You want one?" I ast him, and without waiting for him to answer me, I brung out another glass and poured him a drink.

"Thanks, Marshal," he said, and he picked it up and dranked it down. Just then Doc come a-walking in.

"Barjack," he said. "Happy said you got a shot man in here."

"Let him in the cell, Butcher," I said.

Butcher tuck the keys and opened the cell door and Doc went on inside. Pretty soon I heared the owl hooter yelp. "That looks bad enough," Doc said.

"Well, fix it up for me," the bastard said.

"Barjack," Doc called out, "you got some whiskey out there?"

I picked up my bottle and handed it to Butcher. He tuck it in to Doc, and Doc musta just poured a drink of it out onto the outlaw's leg where my bullet had gone in. I tell you what. That sorry shit really set up a howl then.

"What you going to do, Doc?" I said. "Cut off his fucking leg?"

"I'm thinking about it," Doc said.

"No," shouted that Mac. "No. You ain't gonna cut off my leg. No."

"Butcher," I said, "can you shut that man up?"

Butcher walked back into that cell and slugged old Mac hard on the jaw and knocked him cold.

"Thanks," Doc said.

Happy come in then and said, "Barjack, we're ready out here."

I finished off my drink and stood up. "Doc," I said, "whenever you're all did in there, here's the key to lock that cell back up."

"I'll take care of it, Barjack," he said, and I walked out the front door with Happy and Butcher. Ever'one, even ole Sly, was out there mounted up and ready to go. They was three saddled horses waiting for the three of us. I seed ole Bonnie a-setting on top of a horse that looked like as if he was only just barely big enough to carry her. She was still a-wearing one a' her floozy dresses too, and she did look a riot a-holding on to that Henry rifle. Me and my depit-ties mounted up, and I turned my horse to ride south.

"Churkee," I said, "ride up here alongside a' me. You're the one what knows where we're a-going."

Miller hauled up beside a' me, and we commenced to riding. There was me and Butcher and Happy. Then they was Miller and Sly and Dingle. Final they was the two gals, Bonnie and Polly. So they was eight of us all tole. If we was right about that Cody gang, they was seven a' them out there. So we had them just a little outnumbered, but then two of us was female. Both of them had kilt before, though, so that didn't worry me none too much.

Bonnie rid up beside a' me on the other side from Miller, and I give her a look. I tell you what, she had a hard set and grim look on her round face. "Bonnie," I said, "how come you to want to ride along on a chore like this here?"

"The bastards said they was going to kill you and burn down our town," she said, "including my Hooch House."

"Our Hooch House," I said.

"Hell, Barjack," she said, "I know that."

"Barjack," said Miller, "when we get there, what do we do?"

"If you was right," I said, "they won't suspect nothing when they hear us coming. We'll just ride up as close as we can get and dismount. They'll see who we really is by then, and likely they'll start in to shooting at us, and we'll shoot back. The difference is they'll likely have a fire going, so we'll have a better look at them than what they'll have at us. That's all."

"There's a ridge on the other side a' the road," he said. "It's got good cover."

"Oh yeah? Well, we just might make use of it," I said.

Chapter Eleven

We was riding along slow and easylike, ever'one
was alert, on account a' I had tole them to be in
case some of that seven had decided to ride along
behint the other six, but we hadn't seed no sign a'
no one. Miller pointed up ahead to where the road
kindly swerved around to the right. "They're just
beyond that curve," he said. "On the right side of
the road." I looked and I could see that on the left,
just like he had said, the ground rose up, and it
looked to me like it riz higher the farther along we
would go. I helt us up then.

"Let's get off a' these horses and let them keep
on a-going," I said. "While they're a-walking past
the camp, we'll climb up on that ridge up there."

I led us on till we rounded that curve in the road
and we could see the campfire right where Miller
said it would be. Then we all dismounted and
slapped our horses on their ass so they'd keep on
a-going. Then I led the way to the side a' the road
opposite a' the camp. We all went to climbing. Ever'
now and then one of us would drop off and duck
behind a boulder or a bush there on that slope. Final we was all down. I was hunkered down behint
a rock, which was about half as tall as me. I could

see the men down below and across the road pretty
clear even though it had done turned dark. They
was around a fire. It looked to me like they was
drinking coffee but only one a' them had a bottle he
was passing around. He got his bottle back, and
he was standing up next to the fire and taking a
long drink.

Happy was behint another rock just kindly to
my right, and he was toting his Winchester rifle. I
knowed he was good with it. "Happy," I said, and
he looked over at me. "See can you hit that bottle,"
He raised up that rifle and sighted in. Then pretty
soon, he squeezed the trigger. The bottle exploded
glass and whiskey all over the place, and the whole
damn gang reached for their weapons and went
to looking around for something to shoot back at. I
yelled down at them.

"Throw down your guns and put your hands
up," I said. "Else we'll kill you all."

The one what Miller and Polly was both after,
the one called Cody, he answered me. "Who the
hell are you?"

"I'm Marshal Barjack," I yelled, "and I got me a
posse here a' forty men."

"Yeah? Well, I got men who'll be riding back
here to join up with us at any time now."

"You ain't got no one," I said. "You had six more,
and five of them are dead back in Asininity. The
other'n is in jail getting his one leg cut off. They
never even made it to the front door a' the bank."

"Take cover, men," Cody shouted, and they all
went to diving for gopher holes. Cody, he went diving back behint hisself, and he disappeared. The
rest of them was all down on their bellies, behint

fallen-down trees or hiding behint live standing-up ones or somewheres else. And they was all shooting at us, or they was all shooting at the hill-side where we was at. I don't think any of them was a-coming close to any of us. They couldn't really tell just where we was at. One of them stood up in a crouch and went to running back toward where ole Cody had disappeared at. I tuck a careful aim with my Merwin and Hulbert and snapped off a shot at him, and he yelped and tuck a tumble.

Then Sly stood up and started down the hill, and Miller come right behint him. "What the hell are you two a-doing?" I said, but they never bothered to answer me. They just kept on a-going till they was down in the road, and then they kept on a-walking toward that camp. I seed bullets kicking up dust nearby them both, but they kept a-walking with their guns in their hands. When they got close to the camp, Sly picked out one what was peeking out from around a big tree, and he snapped off a shot and drilled the son of a bitch through the neck. Miller got one what was laying down behint a log. He shot his in the forehead. They kept a-walking, and they walked right past one what was behint a tree, and he stepped out with a gun in each hand, and he aimed at Sly's back, but ole Polly drilled him clean right betwixt the shoulder blades, clean from up on the hillside where she was hid at. They was two of them left, not counting that Cody. One of them jumped and went to running through the woods. The other'n musta been buried low some-wheres. I never seed him atall. Sly and Miller was a-standing in the middle a' that camp a-looking around, but they couldn't find no one.

"Let's all go down," I said, and I stood up and started making my own way. I could hear the rest of them a-follering me. Pretty damn soon we was all down in the road and walking toward Miller and Sly. "Happy," I said, "go see can you catch up our horses." He went running off down the road. I walked up beside a' Miller. "Cody went off thattaway," I said, pointing back behint the campfire. Me and Miller walked back thattaway. There was a sharp drop-off to a little gully, and there was six horses there. "So that's how come him to disappear so quick," I said.

"Damn," Miller said.

Polly come up to us just then and she sized up the situation right quick. "So the son of a bitch got away again," she said.

We walked back to the middle a' the camp, and I looked around. "Where's Bonnie?" I said.

"Oh," Dingle said, "she went running after Happy down the road."

"Goddamn it," I said. "One a' them bastards run through the woods thattaway."

"Look here, Barjack," said Butcher. I looked and he was a kneeling beside a stack a' stuff and he had a bottle in his hand.

"Well," I said, "have a goddamned drink on the bastards."

He uncorked that son of a bitch and tipped it up, taking a long drink. Then he helt it out toward me and I tuck it and had me a drink. I passed it over to Polly. "It ain't the best whiskey I've ever drunk," I said, "but we never paid for it neither."

Polly had herself a snort. Then we heared a shot come from a distance to the south. We all of us looked thattaway with our guns ready. We waited. By and by we heared some horses coming. I walked out into the road, holding my trusty Merwin and Hulbert self-extracting six-shooter ready for anything. But then here come Happy and Bonnie, each one riding a horse. Happy was leading a couple of others.

"What the hell was that gunshot?" I said.

"It was Bonnie what shot it," Happy said.

"What for?"

"That bastard was fixing to shoot Happy," Bonnie said.

"Tell me what the hell happened down there," I demanded.

"Well," said Happy, "I had caught up one horse. It was this one here that I'm a-riding."

"I don't care about that part of it, goddamn it," I said. "Tell me about the shooting."

"Happy was catching up that horse," Bonnie said, "and that no-good son of a bitch stepped out of the woods beside the road and took aim at Happy's back. I was just a little ways back, and I seen him, so I shot him with my rifle. That's all."

"Did you kill the bastard?" I ast her.

"I don't know," she said. "He didn't move none."

"She killed him dead, Barjack," said Happy.

"All right then," I said. "We got them all but 'cept Cody."

Then one a' the ones laying around the campfire went to moaning and wiggling around a little bit. I hurried over to check him. He was shot good, but he weren't dead. I throwed his gun away out of his reach. "Check them others," I said. In another minute, Sly said, "They're all dead, Barjack."

"Happy," I said, "ride back again and see can you catch up the rest of our horses. Butcher, go down in back here and bring up them outlaw horses. Dingle, gether up all a' their weapons."

While Happy was off gathering up our mounts, we got the bodies loaded up on horses and cleaned up the campsite, packing in their gear and putting out the fire, which was some bigger'n it ever needed to be. By the time that was all did, Happy come back with the rest a' the horses and the corpus a' the one Bonnie had kilt down the road. We all mounted up and headed back for Asininity.

When we got back to town it was well into the night, but I told Happy, "You and ole Butcher take these stiffs down to the carnal house, and when you've dropped them off, take all a' the horses to the stable."

"Yes, sir," he said, and him and Butcher headed for the undertaker's. Me and Bonnie, we headed for the Hooch House. Dingle and Polly follered us, but ole Sly the Widdamaker headed for his home. Whenever we stepped inside the Hooch House, I could see right off that Aubrey was having a hell of a time. I guess with me and Bonnie both gone at the same time, some folks decided that the lid was off and anything could go. They was a fight a-going on in one a' the front corners a' the room, and ever'one in the place was hollering around. "Go on back to our table, Bonnie," I said, and she headed for it, follered by Dingle and Polly. I walked toward the fistfight what was under way.

They was five guys involved in it, and I come up behint one of them. He had just picked up a chair to use, but I hauled out my Merwin and Hulbert and whopped him damn hard on top a' his head. He dropped straight down on the floor like a potato sack. Then I aimed my shooter at the middle a' that fight. "Be still, you bastards," I said. They stopped fighting right at once, and they was all a-looking at me. "You think you can break up my place whenever I'm busy somewhere else?"

"No, Barjack," said a cowboy what I knowed. He was a regular customer. He was wiping at some blood on his mouth with a shirtsleeve. "It ain't that. It just—well, it just happened."

Happy and Butcher come in then, and when they seed me with my gun out, they both come right on over. "You're just in time, boys," I said. "Take this bunch to jail, and don't forget that one on the floor."

"Aw, Barjack," said the cowboy.

"Shut up," I said. I holstered my shooter and headed for my table, where I found ole Bonnie a-yelling at someone what was setting at my table. Well, they was a bunch a' someones setting at it. There weren't a single chair available. Bonnie was arguing with someone what had decided to talk up for the rest of them. "What the hell's going on here?" I said.

"These farts are setting at our table, Barjack," Bonnie said.

"I can see that," I said. "All right then. You all might not a-knowed it, but this here table is private. It's reserved. And it's mine, so get up and move somewheres else."

"We got here first, and the table was empty," said the bastard what had been argying with Bonnie.

Well, I didn't want to fuss with him no more, so

instead I tuck hold a' his collar behint his neck and lifted him up outta the chair. Then with my other hand, I pulled the chair out from under his ass, and I dropped him on the floor. I drawed out my six-gun soon as I dropped him, and I pointed it at his head.

"I told you to move," I said. "I own this place along with this lady you was a-fussing with, and on top a' that, I'm the town marshal here. Count yourself lucky I don't throw your ass in jail."

While he was a-standing up, the rest of his buddies was getting up outta their chairs and backing away. The one getting up from the floor looked up into my face, and he said, "Sorry, Marshal. Sorry. I didn't realize." He stood on up, and he tuck his hat in his hands, and he looked at Bonnie. "Sorry, ma'am," he said. Then the whole bunch of them left. They never went to another table nor to the bar. They just left by the front door. I set down in my chair. Aubrey come running with our drinks. Happy and Butcher come back in then, and they come over to the table and set down.

"You get them ole boys locked up safe and sound?" I ast them.

"We sure did, Barjack," Happy said.

"One of them was howling around," said Butcher, "till Happy throwed a' bucket a' water on him."

He went to laughing then. And Happy chuckled some too.

"I wish I had been there to see it," I said.

"I wouldn'ta did it if you'da been there," Happy said.

"How come?"

"I don't know," he said. "I just know I wouldn't'a."

That set me to wondering about ole Happy. I guessed that he felt a whole lot more freer whenever I weren't around. It come to me that if I was around, he wouldn't do nothing without he ast me first if it was all right. I guessed I was just too damn bossy or something. I wanted to say something to him, but I couldn't think just what it was I wanted to say, so instead, I picked up my glass and tuck a big swaller.

"Barjack?" said Butcher.

"Whut?"

"Whenever we was coming back in just now, we passed a bunch a' guys leaving, and they was grumbling around and talking about you it sounded like to me."

"So?"

"I was just wondering what the hell was wrong with them."

"They was setting at our table whenever we come in," said Bonnie, "and Barjack throwed them out."

"Oh," said Butcher. "They was lucky then, I guess."

"What do you mean, Butcher?" Happy ast him.

"Well, if my old man was to walk into his favorite restaurant in the city and find someone sitting at his table, they'd get the shit beat out of them, at least."

"Your old man is a criminal, Butcher," I said. "I'm a lawman. There's a difference."

"I guess so," he said.

Miller the Churkee come in about then, and he come over to set with us. "You've missed some excitement," Bonnie said, and then she went and tole him about the fight what I busted up and the bastards what was a-setting at our table.

"I guess I should've come in with you," he said.

"So where was you?" I ast him.

Aubrey come over and brung him a drink.

"I was just looking after my horse," he said. "I'm thinking about riding after Cody in the morning."

"Again?" I said.

"Yeah. He's alone now."

"But you don't know where he went to," said Happy.

"I can track him," Miller said.

"If you do," said Polly, "I'll go with you."

"What if I don't want you going along?"

"You can't stop me," she said.

"We'll see about that," he said.

I tuck a drink, and I went to studying the both of them. Each one looked damned determined, and if I was to have to bet on one of them, I wouldn'ta knowed which one to bet on.

Chapter Twelve

I never slept very good that night. I was thinking about them two young folks, ole Mose Miller and ole Pistol Polly, a-going out after that goddamned Cody all on their own. I didn't like the sound of it. I tossed around considerable in the bed, but final I did drop off to sleep. I woked up several times in the nighttime, though, and I woked up right early the next morning. I never really give it much thought, but whenever I got my ass outta bed, I got myself dressed right away, being careful not to wake up ole Bonnie, on account a' she might come near killing me if I was to wake her up. Whenever I had all my clothes on and my Merwin and Hulbert self-extracting revolver strapped on around my middle and my hat on my head, I slipped outta the room real quiet like a little goddamned mouse, and I went on down the stairs. Hell, not even ole Aubrey was around yet. It was right early.

I walked all the way down to the livery stable and woked up the man and tole him to get my horse all saddled up and ready to go and bring it down to my marshaling office, and then I walked all the way back down there. I got my Henry rifle ready and stuffed my pockets full a' boxes a' shells.

Then I tuck the bottle outta my desk drawer and put it in my coat pocket. I went to the winder and looked out, wondering what was taking so damn long about getting my horse to me. Final the slow-witted bastard come along with him.

"What tuck you so damn long?" I snapped at him.

"I was all ready to bring him along, when that Indian and that gal come in a-wanting their nags," he said. "I had to get them ready."

"Did they ride on out?" I ast him.

"Soon as they got their crow baits," he said, "they mounted up and lit out."

"Goddamn," I said. I shut the office door and walked on down in the street to my horse.

"You going after them, Marshal?"

"I ain't going for no joyride," I said, swinging my ass up into the saddle. I knowed which way they was headed, so I just tuck out after them. Knowing that they had a start on me, I moved out kinda quicklike. After I had rid along for a ways without no sign of them, I begun to wonder if I had tuck the wrong road, but then I topped a rise and there they was, riding along real calm and easy side by side. They looked for all the world like a couple a' kids out for a pleasant ride together on a Sunday morning. I spurred my old critter to catch up with them.

Whenever they heared my hoofbeats, they turned their heads to see who it was a-coming up behint them. Whenever they recernized me, they stopped to wait for me. I rid up beside them.

"Barjack," said the Churkee. "What brings you along?"

"It don't seem right you two going outta my town after a goddamned outlaw what is wanted for robbing my bank without me along to make it legal-like," I said.

"We told you we were going after him," Polly said, "and you didn't seem to give a damn."

"Well, I slept on it, and I do give a damn. Let's go."

We kicked up our horses and moved out. Nobody said nothing till we come to the outlaws' last camping place, the last place anyone had ever saw that damn Cody, and we stopped there to look the place over. Churkee walked down the slope where Cody had disappeared.

"He grabbed a horse here," he said, "and he lit out that way." He pointed off across the prairie.

"There ain't nothing out that way," I said.

"Well, that's the way he went," Miller said.

"Can you foller his tracks?" I ast.

"All the way to hell," he said.

"Well, shit," said Polly. "Let's get after the son of a bitch."

We mounted up again, and the Churkee led the way, moving slow and watching the trail real careful-like. A time or two he stopped and really studied the ground. Then he'd start up again. Me nor Polly didn't say nothing. We just follered him along real patientlike. Then he stopped his horse and set looking hard at the ground for a bit. He got off and dropped down on one knee. Final he stood up and pointed off to the west where a line a' hills was running north and south. He pointed at them.

"He's headed for those hills," he said.

I looked where he was pointing, and I couldn't see nothing between us and there, "He's done there then," I said.

"Yeah," said Churkee. "Let's go."

The way hills is, they was a lot farther off than they seemed to be. We rid the rest a' that day away and had to make us a camp for the night. We cooked up a mess a' beans and some salt pork, and I pulled the bottle outta my pocket and tuck me a slug a' good whiskey. Then I passed it around. By and by we dropped off to sleep. I swear I thunk I heared a disturbance in the night, but I never really waked up. I just only kinda rolled over and snorted. But whenever I really woked up in the morning, I seed that our horses was gone. All three of them.

"Goddamn it," I yelled out, and Churkee and Polly both come outta their blankets real fast.

"What is it?" Churkee said.

"What?" said Polly.

"Where's our damned horses?" I said.

"They're gone," said Polly.

"Hell," I said, "I can see that. Goddamn it."

"They were secured," said Churkee. "Someone slipped up here and cut them loose."

"That's what happened," said Polly. "It had to be."

"You reckon it was that goddamned Cody?" I ast.

"I'd bet on it," said Miller. "Damn his hide."

"Well, track the son of a bitches," I said. "We'll have to foller them on foot. Damn it to hell. I hate to walk."

"We got no choice," Polly said.

"Cody or whoever it was came up on foot," Churkee said, "probably so he wouldn't make too much noise. Then it looks like he led the horses off. He never just turned them loose."

"Well, let's get going," I said.

We rolled up our bedrolls and throwed them over our shoulders, and Churkee led the way after our horses. We trudged along. It didn't take very long before I was plumb wore out, but just about then, Churkee stopped again.

"Here's where he left his horse," he said. "Then he cut ours loose and led them back here to pick up his own mount. He rode away still leading them."

"He still headed for the hills?" I ast.

"So far," said Churkee.

The little rest made me feel better a bit, so I just said, "Well, okay, let's go."

Churkee tuck the lead again, and me and ole Polly just follered along. It looked to be a hell of a long walk to them hills, and before I knowed it, we had walked away half a' the day. The sun was straight up in the sky, high noon. We stopped and built up a little fire and whomped us up some coffee what had been left behind on account a' we had tuck it out the night before. Our food was all in the saddlebags, and the horse-thieving bastard had tuck the saddles and bags along with the horses. We dranked us some coffee, and I had a few snorts a' the good stuff what was still in my coat pocket. Then I stretched out on the ground, and, oh, but my muscles commenced to aching something fierce. I dropped off to sleep.

I woked up whenever Polly went to shaking me by the shoulder, and I opened my eyeballs up and seed her a-looking down at me. "Whut?" I said. "Barjack," she said, "are you all right?" I tole her a' course I was all right, and then she said, "Are you ready to go?" I got myself up onto my feet, throwed my blanket roll over my shoulders, and the three of us commenced to walking after our horses and that fucking horse thief. I hadn't gone very far before I stumbled and fell right smack down on my face. "Goddamn it," I said. Both a' them youngsters come a-running and kneeled down beside a' me.

"Barjack," said Polly, "are you hurt?"

"No," I said, "just only my pride. I stumbled is all. Help me up."

Well, they each got a' holt a' one a' my arms and lifted me up to my feet, and then I shuck them loose and started in to walking again. "Let's go," I said. I was careful how and where I stepped after that, but my legs was sure as hell hurting. I was thinking that I would likely die before we reached them hills, but I was goddamned determined to see the son of a bitch what had did this to me dead as hell, so I kept alive all right and kept on a-stumbling along. Whenever I felt like as if I just couldn't take another step, I just pulled out my bottle and had me a drink. We kept on a-walking till the sun was low in the sky. I couldn't hardly believe that I had walked a whole entire day long, except that my old bones tole me I had indeed did that. We camped for the night and built a pot a' coffee. My guts was a-grumbling at me on account a' having no food all that day, just liquids was all.

In spite a' my ferocious hungriness, I slept that night. Churkee and Polly tuck turns a-setting up. I couldn't see how come on account a' we didn't have nothing left to steal unless Cody was to slip up on us and steal our guns. Whenever I woked up in the morning, we still had ever'thing we'd had the night before. When I went to set up, I almost couldn't do it. Goddamn, but I was sore. We fixed up some coffee to get us going, but I sure did crave some food. It had been years since I'd had to go a whole day without no food. Anyhow, we dranked up a pot a' coffee and then loaded our ass up with our stuff and went to walking again. I wished that I could just lay down and die, but 'cept I wanted to see that Cody dead too bad to just go on ahead and do it.

We was getting close to the hills whenever Miller spotted a rabbit and shot it. He cleaned it while Polly built a little fire, and then he put the thing on a spit and roasted the little bastard. We coulda used two or three more, but we made it go around for the three of us. Now, I'll tell you whut, I wasn't never too fond a' rabbit meat, but I sure did eat my share a' that little son of a bitch, and what's more, I liked it too. We finished up and packed up and went to walking again. I was all right for a spell on account a' I had et, but by and by I begun to notice all a' my aches and pains again. But we come to the hills, and that made me feel some good again.

But my ole heart sank somewhat whenever I seed Churkee start in to running up that goddamned hillside like a fucking mountain goat. Polly follered him pretty damn good, but I couldn't hardly do it. I tried, but real soon I was on all fours, and it hurted me something awful even to crawl up like I was a-doing. In a bit, Churkee looked back to see me, and he slowed down and waited for me. I made it on where he and Polly was waiting, and I set back on my ass, and I was a-panting like a cur dog what had been chasing a rabbit. The only thing is my

tongue weren't hanging out the way a dog's does.
At least, I don't think it was.

"We'd better sit and rest a spell," said Polly,
a-looking at Churkee. Churkee give me a look.
"Yeah," he said. "I guess so."

I wanted to tell them to go on without me, not to
let me slow them down, but I never. I was too grate-
ful for the suggestion. I just laid back and breathed
hard. I could tell that ole Churkee was anxious to
get going, but he never said nothing. He set down,
but he kept a-looking up the hillside. Final he said,
"You two stay here. I'm going to scout ahead a bit."
He didn't wait for no response from us. He just
tuck out, moving fast up that hillside again. He
was gone in just a minute.

Polly said, "If he finds that damned Cody, I hope
he don't do nothing without coming back for us
first."

"I wouldn't count on it, Pretty Polly," I said. "If
that Churkee gets Cody in his sights, I wouldn't
bet a plugged nickel that Cody'd have another minute to live."

"That bastard," she said. I wondered if she was
talking about Miller or Cody, but I kept my mouth
shut about it. I got myself sorta rested up, and I told
Polly, so we got our ass up and went to climbing after Churkee. She knowed that I was having a rough
time of it, so she went kinder slow, letting me keep
up, We moved along. Pretty soon we come to a place
where the hillside leveled off into a flat field. It was
broad and wide and back behind it, the hills rose up
again. Just as we come up on it, we spied Miller
a-setting there at the edge and looking out. We come
up on him and joined him there.

"What the hell are you doing?" I said.

He gestured ahead, and I looked across the way close to where the hills rose up again, and I seed three horses. They was wearing saddles. They was a good distance off, but I thunk I could recernize them as ours. But there was just only three. So if they was ours, where the hell was Cody and his horse?

"Well," I said, "let's go get them. What are we waiting for?"

"I was kind of waiting to see if Cody would show up," Miller said.

"Even if he does," I said, "there's three of us now. Let's go."

That Churkee jumped up and went to running across that wide-open space. He never said okay or nothing. Whenever I said, "Let's go," he just jumped up and tuck off. I stood up too then, but I sure as hell couldn't run after him. I kinda hobbled along. Polly stayed with me. We had got maybe a third a' the way across, when Churkee had reached the horses. It looked to me like he was looking around to make sure that Cody wasn't nearby and ready to shoot him from an ambush or something like that. Final, he mounted up on one a' the horses and tuck the others by the reins and come riding back toward us. He met us right smack in the middle a' that wide-open space. Now, I can tell you that I was never in my whole entire life so goddamn happy to see a horse as I was just at that moment. I tuck holt a' the reins with a handful a' mane in one hand and grabbed on to the saddle horn with the other'n, but I couldn't seem to get my goddamned foot lifted up high enough to reach the stirrup. "Shit," I said.

"Here, let me help you," said Polly, and she come

over by my side and tuck holt a' my leg just below the knee and lifted it up till I could slip my foot into the stirrup. Damn, it hurted. I winced and pulled myself on up into the saddle, and then I just kinder settled down in it trying to relax and feeling good that I weren't standing on my sorry-ass legs no more.

"Now, Mose," said Polly, "which a-way did Cody go?"

"Just follow me," he said, and he went to riding. We follered him. He never rid back to where he had found our horses. I reckon he had done scouted out the tracks and knowed where he was going. As we moved out, I noticed that the movement of the horse under me caused my aching bones and muscles to hurt again. I was disappointed. I had been thinking that all I needed was to get back in a saddle and ever'thing would be all right. Well, it was better, but it was far from all right. All that time a-walking had ruint me for sure. I figgered that I was crippled for life.

We rid along at a fair clip. I figgered that Churkee was follering tracks, so I just follered him. Polly did too. I squinnied my eyeballs way up ahead of us, but I never seed no sign a' no rider up there. I just kept on a-trusting Churkee's tracking skills. By and by, he slowed down and he studied the ground real careful-like. Then he made a sharp turn, but he turned back east instead a' west. That tuck me by some surprise. I had thought the bastard was headed into the hills, but if Churkee was reading the sign right, he was heading back down outta them. We made our way back down on the flat and into the main road.

"What the hell is this?" I said.

"Cody's headed back to Asininity," said Miller.

"Goddamn it," I said, "I think we're chasing a crazy son of a bitch."

Chapter Thirteen

Well, hell, the sun was long down whenever we got our ass back into town, and we hauled up in front a' the Hooch House and stopped at the hitch rail. Miller was down in the street in a hurry. Polly was right behint him. They had both of them reached the front door and was a-going in, and I was still a-setting in the saddle. By God, my bones and muscles was aching bad. I looked down at the ground, and it sure as hell seemed a long ways down there. I knowed there wasn't no one going to give me a hand in getting down, so I final lifted my ass up and swung my right leg over the back a' my ole nag. Whenever my feet hit the ground, I felt a sharp pain run all the way up my legs and into my spine, and I groaned out loud. Good thing there weren't no one around to hear me. I looped the reins around the rail and turned my ass toward the front door, and it tuck ever'thing I had to amble myself up onto the sidewalk and on into the Hooch House. Whenever I stepped inside, I stopped and looked the place over. Applewhite had hisself a few cardplayers. I needed a little break before I went to walking across that big room.

I seed right off that Polly and Miller the Churkee had done made their way back to my table, and they was setting there with ole Bonnie and Butcher and Happy and Dingle and Sly. Well, I drawed myself up as tall as I could and started in to walking back there as straight and tall as I could muster up. Ever' step hurt, though. I was a-thinking that now I had as much reason for wanting to kill that goddamn Cody as ever Churkee or Polly had, on account a' him stealing our horses was the cause a' my present misery. I made it all right back to my table, and my own personal and private chair was setting empty right beside a' Bonnie, so I pulled it back and set down in it. Bonnie grabbed me right fast and hugged me tight as hell, and goddamn it hurt my sore muscles. Final, after she give me a real slobbery kiss, she turned mostly a loose a' me.

No one ast me no questions, on account a' they had done quizzed up Polly and Miller and got all the answers they wanted about our recent activities. I was hoping they hadn't tole about the episode with our horses. That whole thing was goddamned embarrassing. Now we all knowed that goddamned Cody was somewhere real close by, but Miller had lost his tracks a couple miles outside a' Asininity, so we wasn't atall sure a' where the son of a bitch had went.

"Churkee," I said, "have you tole about tracking that bastard near back here?"

"Yes, I did, Barjack," Miller said.

"Has anyone seed him come into town?" I ast around to ever'one.

Bonnie answered for all of them. "No, Barjack. We ain't seed hide nor hair of him."

"Well," I said, "anyone who sees the son of a bitch, shoot him quick. Then come and tell me about it."

"Yes, sir," said Happy.

"Right now," I said, "I want you, Happy, to go out front and take care of our horses."

"Yes, sir," he said, getting up outta his chair. "Is they all tied up at the rail in front?"

"Where the hell else would they be at?"

"Well, they could be—"

"Oh, shut up, Happy. They're right out front. Go on now."

"Yessir," he said, and he hurried on outta there.

Aubrey brung me a glass a' whiskey. It had tuck him so long on account a' the place was real busy that evening. I picked it up and drunk down about half of it all at once. Damn, it was good. "Bonnie," I said, "do you reckon you could get someone to whup me up something to eat?"

"I reckon so, darlin'," she said, and she stood up and waddled over to where Aubrey was standing behint the bar. Then she come waddling back and set back down. "It'll be right out," she said. She reached around me and give me another slobbery smack on the side a' my face, which I squenched up with a ugly look. Soon as Bonnie turned me a-loose, I picked up my glass and dranked the whiskey the rest a' the way down. I lifted the empty glass up in the air, but ole Aubrey had disappeared. I reckon he was back in the back room seeing to my food. Bonnie stood up again, tuck the glass outta my hand, and headed for the bar with it. In another minute she brung it back all full up again. I had done satisfied my immediate desperate craving, so I just tuck me a little sip.

"Barjack," said Sly.

"What is it, Widdamaker?" I said.

"What do you suppose that Cody came back here for?"

"Your guess is good as mine," I said. "Maybe he's a-looking for revenge. He can't be thinking a' robbing the bank again. He's done lost all a' his bad men trying. Now he's all alone."

"Is there any way he could have sneaked into town without any of us knowing about it?"

"Not much of a one," I said. "He'd have to have someplace to hole up and sleep."

"Widder Rogers has a couple a' rooms available most of the time," Dingle said. "She's kind of on the edge of town."

"He could have stopped there then," said Miller.

"Could have," I said. "We'll check it out in the morning."

"Why not now?" Miller said.

"On account a' I said in the morning."

No one said nothing more about it then. Aubrey brung me a big platter a' steak and taters and some biscuit. "You want any coffee, Barjack?" he ast.

I picked up my whiskey glass. "No, I'm doing just fine," I tole him.

Well, I got myself drunk as a ole crow and let Bonnie drag my ass up the stairs to our room, where she stripped me nekkid and throwed me in bed, and I ain't a-telling what she done to me after that, except to say that it weren't near as much fun as it mighta been if I hadn't a-been so damned drunked up and so all-fired sore from all that damned walking. To tell you the truth, I don't rightly remember it none too well nohow. Even so, I still woked up early enough in the morning.

Bonnie was still a-snoozing, and I got me dressed as quiet as I could and slipped out the door. I stopped downstairs and had Aubrey fetch me out a breakfast and a cup a' coffee and a glass a' whiskey, and I had just about finished up whenever Happy and Butcher come in. I let them get some breakfast, and then I told 'em let's go. They got up and follered me out to the street. Happy said, "Where we going, Barjack?" I never answered him. I just kept on a-walking and they kept on a-follering me. I led them all the way down to the end a' the street to where the Widder Rogers's place was at. I walked up to the front door, and my two dumb-ass depitties walked up right behint me. I knocked. In a minute the door was opened by the widder.

"Good morning, Barjack," she said. "What kin I do fer you?"

"Morning, Miz Rogers," I said. "I'm a-wondering, did you get a new guest recent?"

"Why, yes, I did. Name a' Jones."

"Is he still here?"

"Well, he ain't here just now, but then again, he ain't checked out neither. Has he did something wrong, Marshal?"

"I'm just doing some routine checking up is all," I said. "Can I look in his room?"

"Come on," she said, and she led the way and I follered and Butcher and Happy follered me. She unlocked the room and the three of us walked in.

She stayed out in the hallway. First off, I just stood and kinder looked around. A pair a saddlebags was throwed on a chair, and a blanket roll was tossed on top a' the bed. The bed had been slept in and hadn't been made since. I pointed at the roll and said to Happy, "Unroll that and check it out." While he was a-undoing the bedroll, I went and looked in the saddlebags.

"Clean clothes is all," Happy said.

There wasn't nothing in the saddlebags to give us no clue neither. I walked back out and ast the widder, "Can you describe this Jones?"

She said, "Well, I think he's about as tall as Happy there, and he has reddish hair and a droopy mustache. Kind of a little potbelly. He's a nice-enough-looking feller, though. I can't think of nothing else."

"Thank you, ma'am," I said. "Let's go, boys."

But whenever we got outside, I tole Happy to find hisself a place to lurk around and watch for that damned Cody should he come back to his room.

Me and Butcher walked back to the Hooch House, and when we went in, I looked over the crowd real good, but a' course, I never seed that Cody. Applewhite was dealing cards in his corner table. Before we had made it back to my table, I heared a commotion and looked around. Two of the cardplayers had knocked over their chairs and pulled six-guns. They commenced to shooting at each other.

"You goddamned cheat," one of them yelled.

"I ain't, you son of a bitch," said t'other'n.

"You're calling my mama names," said the first one.

They was punctiating their words with gunshots.

The noise was terrible inside, and the air was being filled up with the foul smell of burnt black powder. Butcher headed for the card table right fast, and I ambled my way after him. I counted twelve shots, what meant that each a' the damn fools had full loaded their pieces. I call them fools on account a' only a fool would full load a six-gun. Anyone with any brains leaves one empty chamber under the hammer. Them two was standing right across the table from each other, and twelve shots was fired and no one in the whole damn place, not even the shooters, was hit once.

Butcher stepped up right behint the nearest one and whopped him hard over the head with his shooter, and then done the same thing to the other one. It sounded like as if someone had dropped one flour sack right after another one whenever they hit the floor. "All right," I said, "get them on over to the jail and lock them up." Butcher recruited a couple a' the customers to help, and they hauled the bastards out. I went back and set down right next to ole Bonnie, and Aubrey already had me a drink set up. I tuck it up right away and had me a slurp.

"Who was they?" I ast Bonnie.

"I don't know, Barjack," she said. "I think they're local, though. I think I seen them in here before."

"They weren't good shots," said Dingle. He was a-scribbling as usual.

"What the hell are you a-writing, Scribbler?" I ast.

"Just taking notes is all, Barjack," he answered. "I don't have a new story line yet."

I drank down about half a' my whiskey, and ole

Peester come a walking in. It was a kinder unusual thing for our esteemed mayor to grace our establishment. Ole Bonnie stood up and give him a real big smile and said, "Mr. Mayor Peester, welcome. Come on over here and set with us." Peester come on over, and Bonnie pulled him out a chair, and he set in it. She waved at Aubrey and he come over to see what the pettifogging mayor might want. I ordered him a shot a' my own favorite whiskey, and he never argued none, so Aubrey brung it to him.

"Well, Mr. Pisster," I said, "what the hell brings you in here?"

He tuck a sip a' whiskey and went to coughing. Final he got over it, and he looked up at me. There was tears in his eyes. "Sorry, Barjack," he said. "What did you ask?"

"I ast you what is it that brings you in here?"

"Oh," he said. "Oh yeah. Well, old moneybags over at the bank has put up a reward for that bank robber you've been chasing."

"He has, has he? Sounds like he don't trust me to run the son of a bitch down."

"Oh no. It's not that. You can collect the reward yourself, if you get the man."

"Is it dead or alive?" I ast.

"Dead or alive," he said.

"How much?"

"Two hundred dollars."

"That ain't so much," I said.

"Maybe not to a rich man like you," Peester said, "but it's a lot of money to most folks in these parts."

"Well, hell," I said, "maybe I'll just let one a' them get the son of a bitch and collect all a' that loot then."

"As long as he gets got," Peester said. "That's all we care about."

"We'll get him all right," I said. "Don't worry about that none."

"What makes you so sure?"

"Why, shit, your orneriness," I said, "he's in town right now."

"He's what?"

"We know that for sure."

"Right here? Right in town? Now?"

"That's the gospel truth."

"Why aren't you out arresting him?"

"I don't know exact where he's at."

"But you know he's in town?"

"That's right, your mayorness. You see, we was out tracking him, and his tracks swung around and led us right back here. In fact, I know for sure and certain that he's been a-staying down with the Widder Rogers."

"Go down there and get him," said Peester.

"Now, stop your shouting," I said. "I done went down there and he was out."

"Well—well, do something."

"I'll just let that ree-ward take care a' the problem," I said.

"That's no attitude for you to take," Peester blubbered. "You're the law here, and it's your job to apprehend that—that—what's his name?"

"Harm Cody is what he calls hisself, when he ain't calling hisself Jones."

"Well, Harm is a good name for him. It's your job to apprehend him, reward or no reward."

"All right, Peester," I said, "since it's my job, let me worry about it. Let me do it my own way, and you cut out interfering with me in the line a' my duty."

"You just be sure that you get him," Peester said. "And soon."

He drank down the rest a' his whiskey and stood up to leave. I kinder stuck my leg out so that he would trip over it, and he did for sure, sprawling out on the floor on his face. He yelped whenever he fell down. I stood up and reached down to help him back up onto his feet.

"Be careful, Mr. Mayoralty," I said. "You might could hurt yourself thattaway."

He got on up and give me a dirty look. "You just remember what I said," he tole me, and he stomped the whole way across the room and out the front door. If he coulda slammed the swinging doors, he woulda. He did run smack into Happy as him and Butcher was coming back in. Bonnie slugged the shit outta my shoulder.

"Ow," I said. "What the hell was that for?"

"You tripped him over on purpose," she said.

"So what?"

"He's our mayor, Barjack."

Chapter Fourteen

"Where the hell could that son of a bitch be hiding out in my town?" I ast myself out loud.

"You talking about that Harm feller?" Bonnie said.

"What?" I said, on account a' I never even realized I had been talking out loud.

"You was wondering where someone could be hiding," she said. "Was you talking about Harm Cody?"

"Oh. Yeah," I said. "I can't figger how the son of a bitch could be right here in town and no one know where the hell he's at. He's got hisself a room down to the Widder Rogers's place, but he ain't in it."

"There ain't many places to hide out in town," Bonnie said.

"I left ole Happy to watch the damn place," I said.

"Well, Happy'll get him, Barjack," Bonnie said. "He'll have to go back to his room sometime. Won't he?"

"You never know about a snake like that," I said. "He might crawl back in the same hole he come out of and he might not."

I got to thinking real hard, and when I done that,

I got to asking myself how come him to come back into Asininity in the first damn place. Ole Miller had said that he wanted revenge on me. Maybe so, I thunk. But maybe so, he also wanted to get rid of that Churkee, and maybe so he also wanted that there bank money what my posse had tuck back from him. So there was the bank money and me and Churkee. Well, ole Churkee come walking in just then too, and he come on back to my table to set down. Aubrey brung him a drink.

"Churkee," I said, "I been thinking 'bout what you said about that Cody coming back here to town. If he comes a-looking for you or for me, I think we had ought to be together. So I want you to stick close to me from here on. Least, till we get his ass."

"All right, Barjack," he said. "That makes sense to me. But what if he goes for the bank instead of going for one of us?"

"Butcher here is going to watch the bank," I said.

"I am?"

"You damn right you are. Starting right now. Find yourself a hidey-hole where you can watch the bank and stay there till you either gets Cody or I come and tell you to quit."

"Yes, sir," said Butcher, and he got up and left outta the Hooch House in a hurry.

That left me and Churkee setting together but across the table from each other, so he was a-looking one way, and I was looking the other way. I couldn't think a' nothing else what could be did unless it would be for us to get organized and go from one house and building in town to another till we had searched the whole damn thing, and that didn't quite make sense to me. I even wondered if it would even a' been a legal thing for me to do, busting in on folks in their own homes. So I never even mentioned that possibility to no one else.

I emptied down my drink glass and waved at ole Aubrey, and he come a-running with the bottle. And just as he poured my glass full again, we heared a shot what come from someplace real close outside. Aubrey jumped and like to've dropped my bottle. Bonnie didn't exactly scream, but she said, "Oh," kinda sharplike. Me and Miller both of us come up out of our chairs with six-guns in our hands. We looked at each other and then toward the front door.

"Let's go," I said.

We headed toward the front a' the place and then on outside. We stood there on the sidewalk and looked down the street both ways. Then Butcher hollered from up on a rooftop across the street from the bank.

"Barjack," he said, "around the corner."

He was a-waving north, so me and Miller went running thattaway to the next corner and then on around it. We never had far to go, though, on account a' once we had went around the corner, we seed a body a-laying out in the road. We both of us looked down the street, but we never seed a damn thing. We walked on up to where the body was stretched out. It was laying on its face, and its back had a big hole blowed in it. I walked on over to it and nudged it over with my foot, and whenever it flopped on over, I could see right off that it was poor ole Harry Henshaw.

"Murdered," I said.

"Harm Cody?" said Miller.

"I'd say so," I tole him. "Henshaw was in the posse."

"Yeah," said Miller. "If he thought that Henshaw was that important, then he must be after you and me."

"I'd damn well bet money on it," I said.

We walked back around to the main street, where I yelled at a couple a' fellers and tole them to go tell the undertaker to get down there and take care a' the stiff, and then we walked back down the side street where the body was still a-laying. We walked past it and on down the street a-looking for any place Cody coulda gone. We went slow and looked into every nook along the way. We had our shooters our in our hands too, just in case. But we not only never seed no sign a Cody, we never seed no place where he coulda gone to.

We had moved about halfway down that side street when we heared a loud crash like as if someone had stumbled over a bunch a' boxes. We pressed ourselfs back against the wall and helt our shooters ready. Nothing happened. I looked over at Miller, and I nodded ahead. We tuck off together at a run, and we come to a sunk-in doorway, and we both of us poked our gun barrels in there at the same time. Ole Jake Jacobson looked up at us with his bleery eyes opened real wide. He sure enough looked skeered to death.

"Don't shoot me, Marshal. Mr. Indi'n. Please don't shoot."

"Jake," I said, "what the hell are you a-doing here?"

"I just seen a man shot, Marshal," he said, "and I ducked in here to hide. I think he was killed. The man I seen shot, that is."

"He was killed all right," I said. "It was Harry Henshaw."

"Harry was killed?" Jake said.

"Deader'n hell," I said.

"Aw."

"Now, just what did you see, Jake?"

"You ain't gonna shoot me?"

"No," I said, "we ain't gonna shoot you, although we might be doing you a favor if we was."

"Or take me to jail?"

"No, now, what did you see?"

"Well, sir," he said, "I was just a-walking down the street here thissaway, and I seen old Henshaw a-coming kinder toward me, but I don't think he seen me, and then someone stepped out in the street behind him and shot him. I jumped into this here doorway right quick, and the shooter went running down the street right past me and around the corner—thattaway."

"He went around to the right?" said Miller.

Jake stepped out of the doorway and faced the corner he had designated. He helt up both a' his hands and looked at them. "Yeah," he said, "to the right."

"Then he never seed you?" I said.

"I reckon not," said Jake, "but it for sure skeered me whenever I fell over them boxes. I never even seen them till then. And then I seen your guns, and I like to've shit my pants, but I never."

"Thank the Lord God for small favors," I said.

"Well, you go on and find the W.C. before you get yourself in real trouble."

"Yes, sir, Marshal," Jake said. "Oh yeah. It was that fellow Cody." He was already running toward the outhouse. He called out over his shoulder as he ran, "That's who it was. That Cody."

As Jake disappeared around the corner, Miller and I looked at each other.

"It was Cody all right," Miller said. "Shall we follow him?"

"Let's go," I said. We walked down to the end of that block and peered around the corner. We didn't see no sign a' Cody, so we went on around the corner to the right, just like Jake had told us. We went slower then, and we looked in ever' doorway and tried ever' door. If the door weren't locked, we opened it up and ast whoever was in there if anyone had come in the last several minutes. They all said no, so we just kept on a-going. Then we come to a dry goods store, and the door was unlocked. We went in. The proprietor was there. It was ole Hardcase Haggerty.

"Well, hello, Marshal," Haggerty said. "What can I do fer you?"

"I'm looking for a man," I said. "Name a' Cody, 'cept only he's a-calling hisself Jones right now."

"What's he look like?" Haggerty ast.

Miller give him a quick description, and then Hardcase said, "Yeah. He come in here, and then he hurried right on out the back door." He turned and pointed to it.

"Come on, Churkee," I said, and we hurried through the back door. Then we was standing there in the goddamned alley a-looking up and down. We was right back behind the Hooch House.

"He could've gone anywhere," Miller said.

"You're right," I said. "Hell, let's go on in the Hooch House and have a drink."

He said, "Okay," and we went on in through the back door. The place was crowded, but all the gals was downstairs except one. We set down at my table with Bonnie and Dingle and Aubrey brung us our drinks. I tuck a slug out a mine, and then I said to Bonnie, "Where's Hot Pants Harriett? She get herself some man business?"

"Yeah," said Bonnie. "They went upstairs just a few minutes ago."

"Well, hell, I hope they're having a damn good time," I said, "but even more, I hope he's got plenty a' cash on his ass."

"Was he a good-looking young fellow?" Miller said.

"I didn't hardly even see the man," said Bonnie. "I just seen Harriett take a fellow by his arm over yonder at the foot a' the stairs and then they headed up. He was a little on the heavy side, I think, but that's all I can say about him."

I just barely noticed the look on Miller's face. It was a look a curiositiousness if I ever did see one. He was a-looking at ole Bonnie, but then he turned and looked at the stairway. He was a-studying it like as if he had never seed it before. Then he turned and looked back at Bonnie.

"Where was Harriet standing before she got hold of that man?" he asked her.

"Oh, I ain't sure," Bonnie said. "I guess she was standing back yonder by the stairs. I can't remember that for sure. How come you want to know that?"

"Barjack," Miller said. "Look back there. See how close the stairway is to the back door?"

"Yeah. So what?" I said.

"So if a man came through the back door and wanted a hiding place and found a gal standing right there handy, what would be the smart thing for him to do?"

Well, I wasn't none too swift nor too smart, but I went and looked at the back door and then at the bottom a' the stairway, and I went and tried to picture ole Harriett a-standing there, and then I pictured ole Cody coming through the back door and walking right up to Harriett. I looked back at Miller, and then the both of us stood up together and walked to the stairs.

"What room?" he ast me as we was a-climbing.

"Any room 'cepting mine," I said.

We hustled on up them stairs, and back downstairs I could hear Bonnie calling after us.

"What the hell are you two up to?" she yelled.

"Never mind," I hollered back.

Then me and ole Miller reached the top a' the stairs, and then we seed old Harriett a-coming toward us. We hurried up to meet her.

"Where is he?" I demanded.

"Who?" she said.

"Who the hell do you think?" I said. "The son of a bitch you was with. That goddamned Cody."

"His name was Jones," she said. "I called him Jonesy."

"Well, he's Cody," I said.

"Where is he?" said Miller.

"Well, he left."

"Already?" I said.

"Wham, bam, thank you, ma'am," said Harriet. "He left by that door."

She jerked a thumb over her shoulder toward the door at the end of the hallway. It led out onto a balcony that had a stairway that led down to the alley behind the Hooch House. We nearly knocked poor ole Harriett down running past her to the door.

"What the hell?" she said.

Miller beat me to the door by several steps. He jerked it open and went on out onto the balcony. I come up behint him. We both of us stood up there looking around, but we never seed nothing a' the bastard.

"I bet he run to the main street," I said. "Come on."

We hurried on down the stairs and out to the main street. It was crowded. We stopped and stared up and down the street, looking for that son of a bitch, but we never seed nothing of him. Not a damn thing. How the hell anyone could appear and disappear in a small place like Asininity just boggles my pea brain. I never seed nothing like it before nor since. We walked on out onto the street, and looking all around us, walked down to the front door a' the Hooch House and went on back in and over to my table, where we set back down.

"What the hell was that all about?" Bonnie said.

"That was all about trying to run down that god-damn Cody bastard," I said.

"Cody?" she said.

"That's right," I said.

"He killed Henshaw outside around the corner," Miller said. "We followed him around the next corner, where he went into the dry goods store and out the back door."

"Then it sure looks like he come into our back door and found ole Harriett a-standing near the stairs."

"He just grabbed on to her," said Miller, "and took her upstairs."

"And then wham, bam, thank you, ma'am, and he went out by the balcony. We lost him again."

Chapter Fifteen

I was setting drinking my whiskey and muttering to myself. I was so pissed off that I never even noticed that ole Pistol Polly had come up behint me. "Goddamn it to hell," I said.

"What's the matter with Barjack?" Polly said to Bonnie.

"Aw, him and Miller just missed getting that Cody again," Bonnie said.

Polly hustled on around to the other side a' the table and set down right beside a' Miller with ole Dingle on her other side. "Barjack," she said. "What happened?"

"Shit," I said.

"Mose?" Polly said.

"Aw, we were sitting right here, and we heard a shot, so we went out to investigate. We found that Henshaw shot to death, and we found that drunk, Jake, who saw Cody running away. We ran after him, and we followed him through a store. He went out the back door and came in the back door here. He got one of the whores and went upstairs with her. When we figured that out, we went upstairs after him, but he was already finished and had left by the outside door upstairs."

"Wham, bam, thank you, ma'am," I said.

"Goddamn it," Polly said.

"I'm just having the goddamnedest time figgering out how the son of a bitch can be right here in town in broad daylight right under our goddamned noses, killing folks and fucking gals, and us not being able to even get our damned eyeballs on him."

"He's a smooth one, Barjack," Polly said. "Don't take it too personal."

"It's my damn town," I said. "I got to take it personal. Ain't no other way to take it."

"Well," Polly said, "what the hell are you going to do about it?"

"I got a man on a roof a-watching the town. He can see most of it from up there," I said.

"Let's search the whole damn place," she said.

"We tried that once."

"Obviously it didn't work," said Polly. "Let's do it again."

"All right, by God. Ever' one a' you is deputized. Let's go right now."

"Me too?" said Bonnie.

"You goddamn right," I said.

We all of us stood right up and headed outta the place. Out on the sidewalk I tole them all which part a' the town to take, and we split up. Me and ole Bonnie headed down toward the Widder Rogers's place. Whenever we got there, I knocked on the door. In a minute, the ole widder opened up the door to us.

"Barjack," she said when she seed me, "what are you doing back here?"

"We need to check out your place one more time," I said.

"You still looking for Mr. Jones?"

"Yes, ma'am," I said, " 'cept only his right name is Cody."

"I don't know nothing about that," she said, "but you can go check his room again if you insist on doing it."

"We will," I said, and me and ole Bonnie pushed our way past the widder and on into the house. I led Bonnie the way to the room Cody had been occupying, and we went in. It looked just the same as it had looked the other time I checked in there. "Let's check all the other rooms too," I said, so we went through the whole house. One room we went in had a man asleep in the bed, and he jumped up and looked at us with his eyeballs wide-open.

"What's the meaning of this?" he said.

"That ain't him," I said, and we went back outta the room.

The other rooms was all empty. We was headed back toward the front door whenever we walked past the only door we hadn't opened, and I heared a sound come from in there. It sounded to me like as if someone was lifting a winder up to open it. I jerked my head toward that door.

"What was that?" I said.

"What?" said the widder. "I didn't hear nothing."

"What's this room?" I ast her.

"That's my private bedroom," she said.

"I need to look in there," I said, and I reached for the doorknob. The widder stepped in to block my way.

"No one goes in there," she said.

"I'm a-going," I said, and Bonnie tuck hold a' the widder and pulled her back outta my way. I opened the door and stepped in. The winder was wide up. I hurried on over to it and stuck my fool head out, and I seed that goddamn Cody a-running. He looked over his shoulder and seed me, and he sent a shot back at the winder, I ducked just as his bullet hit the winder frame and sent some splinters a-flying. "Goddamn it," I yelled.

Bonnie come a-running into the room. "Barjack," she yelled. "Are you hit?"

"I'm all right," I said. "He's out there."

I went to climbing through the winder, but by the time I got my fat ass out, he had done disappeared down the street and around a corner. I fired three shots into the air, and Bonnie come a-running around the house. She had went out the front door. "Where'd he go?" she ast me.

I gestured ahead with the barrel a' my gun. "He went thattaway, but I lost him."

"Come on," she said, and she tuck off after the son of a bitch. I follered her. Just then Polly come a-running with Miler alongside of her.

"Was that you signaling?" Miller ast.

"It was," I said. "He went running off thattaway."

The four of us went after him, but whenever we rounded that corner, we seed all kinds a' folks out on the street but no goddamn Cody. We went to searching buildings again, but we never found him. Final we give it up.

"Come on," I said. By that time, Happy and Dingle was with us. I led the way back to the widder's house and never bothered to knock this time. I just barged on in, and they all follered me. The widder stepped up all huffylike.

"What are you a-doing?" she demanded.

"We come back here to take your ass to jail, Widder," I said.

"On what charge?" she said.

"Harboring a goddamned fugitive," I said. "That was that damned Cody hiding in your room."

"I don't know what you're talking about," she said.

"Listen, Widder," said Bonnie. "You had Cody hiding in your private room. You was prob'ly doing more with him than hiding him. Anyhow, he damn near shot my Barjack, so you just as well fess up, damn you."

"I ain't got nothing to fess up to," the widder said.

Bonnie hauled out her Merwin and Hulbert self-extracting .38-caliber revolver and aimed it right between the widder's eyes. "Oh yeah?" she said. "You'd best think about that, you goddamn bitch."

"Now, Bonnie," I said, "put that thing away. There ain't no need for that."

"But she's—"

"We'll just lock her up in the jailhouse," I said. "Come on, Widder. You're under arrest."

"I ain't going to no jail," she said.

"You damn sure are," I said. "Happy, take her along."

Happy stepped up to the widder and helt out a hand. "Come along, ma'am," he said.

She smacked him hard across the face. "I said I ain't a-going."

Bonnie had done had enough a' the bullshit. She was still a-holding out her revolver, and she all of a sudden bashed the widder on top a' the head and dropped her like a sack a' wheat down onto the floor. "Take her on, Happy," she said. Happy commenced to struggling with the deadweight a' the widder, but he was having a hell of a time. Bonnie bent over and hefted the widder up onto her own shoulders. "Come on," she said, and she walked all the way to my marshaling office like that with Happy running along beside of her. I strolled along behind. By the time I stepped into the office, Bonnie had done throwed the widder into a cell, and Happy was locking the door. Bonnie turned on me whenever I come in.

"Well," she said, "what now?"

"We'll question her again whenever she wakes up," I said. "That is, unless you kilt her."

"Aw, hell," said Bonnie, "I never hurt her none."

The rest a' my depitties come into the office then and kindly crowded around me.

"What now?" said Dingle.

"Has you all searched the whole damn town?" I ast them.

"We did," said Miller, "but you found him, and he ran away again. He could be hidden in someplace where we already looked."

"Goddamn it," I said. "You're right about that, a' course. All right, let's go back where I lost him."

We all of us made our way back to the backside a' the widder's house, and I was about to lead the way a-follering the way Cody had went, but a thought come into my head. "A couple a' you check ever' room in the widder's house again," I said. Happy and Miller run into the widder's place by the back door. They come out again in a few minutes a-shrugging, so I said, "Come on," and I led them all around the corner where I had seed him go. The first place we come to was a empty building what had once been a saloon years ago before I closed down all a' my competition. It had never sold, and it was boarded up. "Kick down the door," I said. "We'll check it out."

Happy and Miller went to banging at the door trying to knock it open, and after they had hit it several times, Bonnie shoved them aside. "Get outta the way," she said. They stepped aside, and Bonnie walked up close to the door and turned her back on it. Then she give it a hell of a bump with her incredibly broad ass and knocked it plumb down. She stepped outta the way, and I walked in, my shooter out in my hand. I looked around, but I never seed no one. The others follered me in.

"Look the place over," I tole them, and they went to looking. Happy went behind the old bar. Polly opened the door into the back room. Bonnie and Miller climbed the stairs, and I could hear them opening up and shutting doors up there. By and by they was all back down with me. "The place is clean, Barjack," said Happy.

We went back out into the street and checked the next building. It was the milnery shop or whatever you call it. No sign a' Cody. We went to the next one. It was Henshaw's gun shop. Course, it was closed up on account a' Henshaw being dead, you know. Bonnie opened that door too, and we looked it over real good. Didn't find nothing, so we went back out. We crossed a side street and headed for the stable. The stable man seed us a coming, and I reckon that most ever'one in town knowed by then what we up to. He run outta his place and headed for the Hooch House, so we just walked right in. The place seemed deserted 'cept for the horses what was in there.

"Look in ever' stall," I said.

I walked to the office and opened the door. It was a little bitty thing, so I never even had to step all the way inside to see that there weren't no Cody hiding in it. I went back out and shut the door. My gang a' depitties was just finishing up looking in all the stalls. They come a-walking back to join me. I was looking up at the loft. It was long, running the whole damn length a' the building, and there was bales a' hay stacked up in there. There was a ladder at each end.

"Happy," I said, "climb up that there ladder."

"Yes, sir," he said, and he hurried over to it.

"Miller," I said, and I nodded toward the other ladder. Miller trotted down to it and started in to climbing it. I hauled out my Merwin and Hulber, holding it ready and watching the loft up overhead. Happy was getting close to the top a' his ladder, and just then I seed a bale a' hay come a-toppling toward him. I yelled out, but only I was a little late. "Look out, Happy," I hollered, and I sent a slug up into the loft. I only hit in the stack a' hay, but the one bale come down and clipped ole Happy's head, knocking his hat off and toppling him off a' the ladder. He come a-crashing down to the ground at the bottom a' the ladder. I heared the breath whoosh outta his lungs. I also heared footsteps a-thumping across the boards a' the loft.

Miller hurried on up into the loft with his gun in his hand, and ducking low, he run toward the other end a' the loft. I seed him raise his shooter and snap off a shot. "Outside," he yelled. I went running for the front door. Polly and Bonnie and Dingle run too, and Polly got there before the rest of us. She fired a couple a' shots. Whenever I had reached the door there wasn't no sign a' Cody out there. Up above, Miller reached out from the overhead door what was used for loading up hay bales into the loft. He reached for the rope that was hanging there from a hoist and he tuck hold a' that rope and slid down to the ground.

"Is that how he got down?" I ast.

"Yes, sir," Miller said.

"Goddamn him," I said. "The son of a bitch is slippery as a eel."

I walked back inside to check on ole Happy, and he was just getting up off a' the ground and still sucking for his breath.

"You ain't kilt, are you?" I ast him.

He picked up his hat and dusted it off against his leg. "No, sir," he said. He sucked in another breath. "I'm all right. Was it Cody?"

"I never seed him," I said.

"It was him all right," said Miller. "I caught a glimpse of him."

"Did you hit the son of a bitch?" I said.

"No," said Miller. "I don't think so."

"Do we try to follow him again?" said Bonnie.

"We sure as hell do," I said. "Let's go."

Ole Happy was motivating okay, so I didn't worry no more about him. I let Miller lead the way on account a' he was the only one what seed Cody this time. We went walking through the crowds on the street. Peester was walking in the opposite direction, and when he come up to me, he said, "Barjack. I heared shots fired in town. What's going on?"

"We're a-chasing that goddamned Cody, Pister," I said. "Don't bother me right now. We got us a killer in the streets a' Asininity. Get a gun and join us if you want to."

"Uh, no, Barjack. I think I'll get back to my office."

Chapter Sixteen

Well, we searched all the rest a' that day but never seen hide nor hair a' the son of a bitch. To this here day, I don't know how in the hell he managed to disappear thattaway. If I was to want to be a god-damned criminal, I sure would wish that I could do that. I don't know. Maybe if I was to put my mind to it, I could learn how. I had learnt to fly, you know. That time ole Bonnie had got real pissed off at me and throwed me headlong off a' the landing down into the main room a' the saloon at the Hooch House, I had hovered there in the midair for a spell before I went on down and crashed face-first on a table. I broke my nose that time on account a' it was my first time to fly, and I hadn't yet learnt how to land real good. But recalling that day, I figger that maybe I could learn how to disappear if I was to really put my mind to it.

I didn't sleep real well that night, partly on account a' I didn't have enough whiskey to drink. We had spent nearly the whole damn day a-hunting for that disappearing fart Cody. I don't reckon no one slept good that night thinking about that killer what was loose on our streets. Anyhow, I was sure damn glad whenever morning come and I could get outta bed and get my ass dressed and get on down the stairs. Bonnie was a-snoring when I left the room. Aubrey seed me coming down, and he met me with a cup a' coffee and a glass a' whiskey. I was sure glad to get the whiskey and I drunk it down in a hurry and waved for more. Aubrey brung it to me. Then I sipped at the coffee some and called for a breakfast. Happy and Butcher come in then.

"Has you had your breakfast yet, boys?" I ast them.

"No," said Happy.

"I ain't," said Butcher.

I called out to Aubrey to take care a' them, and then I said to Butcher, "Eat your breakfast up, Butcher, and then go back up on the rooftop and keep an eye out for that goddamned Cody bastard."

"Yes, sir," Butcher said.

"What about me, Barjack?" said Happy.

"You stick with me," I said.

"Okay."

Aubrey final brought out the breakfasts, and we all et them up. Then ole Bonnie come down the stairs, surprising the hell outta me. I reckon that she, like me, didn't sleep none too well. She give me a big squeeze and said, "Good morning, lover."

"Set down, Bonnie," I told her, and she set and waved at Aubrey. He brung her a coffee and a drink, and she called for a breakfast. Butcher wolfed his down and excused hisself and headed out to climb back up on the roof.

"Barjack," Bonnie said, "what are we going to do about that Cody bastard today?"

"I done sent ole Butcher back up on a rooftop to

watch out for him," I said. "I'll think about what else to do."

Miller come walking in just then, and he had Pistol Polly alongside of him. Whilst they was walking toward the table, Bonnie kinder whispered into the side a' my head, "I think them two is developing a interest in each other, Barjack. What do you think?"

"I don't know," I said, "and I don't give a shit."

They come on over and set down on the other side a' the table. In another minute Dingle come in. Whenever he set down, he right away hauled out his damned notebook and went to scribbling in it. I figgered he was making notes 'bout what had went on the day before, but I never bothered to ask him. He never said no good mornings to none of us nor nothing else. He just set his ass down and went to scribbling. Then I was surprised to see ole Sly the Widdamaker come in. He come over and joined us.

Aubrey brung him some coffee. "Would you like a breakfast, Mr. Sly?" Aubrey ast him.

"No, thank you, Aubrey," the Widdamaker said. "I've had my breakfast."

I figgered he had et over at Miss Lillian's fancy house, but I just kept my mouth shut. Sly sipped his coffee.

"Barjack," he said, "do you have any news about Cody?"

"Only that the son of a bitch can disappear into thin air," I said. "We damn near had his ass three or four times yesterday, and he just vanished on us. I never seed nothing like it in all a' my borned days."

"So you think he's still in town?"

"I'm pretty damned sure about that," I said.

"He had been staying at the Widder Rogers's place," said Happy, "but we found him out there."

"Oh, hell, Happy," I said. "You just reminded me that we locked up the widder. Get some breakfast from ole Aubrey and take it on down to her. We can't have no one saying that we starves women in our jailhouse."

"Yes, sir, Barjack," Happy said. "Right away." And he jumped up and headed for the bar.

"Well, he has to be someplace," Sly said.

"If you got any idees about that," I said, "I'm a-listening. We searched the whole damn town. Twice."

"Did you miss any place?" he ast me.

"Just only the place where he was a-hiding," I said. "No. Hell. We went through ever' house and ever' place a' business in town."

"That's strange," he said.

"We come on him in the stable once," I said, "but he got out and disappeared. Then he went upstairs right here with one a' Bonnie's gals, and we just missed his ass by a minute. He went and disap peared again."

"Perhaps he's changing his appearance," Sly said.

"He looked the same each time we got us a glimpse of him," I said, "but I s'pose that's a possibility. He could shave his face and change his clothes, and we'd never know him. Ain't none of us never got a good long look at him."

"I have," said Polly.

"Me too," said Miller. "I'd know him anywhere in any clothes."

"Did the two of you help in the search yester-day?" ast Sly.

"We damn sure did," said Miller.

"And you never saw him?"

"I saw him all right," Miller said, "but then he disappeared."

He sounded almost embarrassed when he said that last word.

"That's right," Polly added.

"There's got to be a way to locate him," Sly said.

"You'd damn well think so," I agreed.

"Do you have any plans for today?"

"Not yet," I said. "Only just posting ole Butcher up on a rooftop is all, and I done done that already."

"Well, let's go," Sly said, pushing back his chair and standing up.

"Again?" I said. "Right now?"

"Do you know a better time?"

"I reckon not," I said, and I got up too. Then ever'one else done the same thing. We all walked out the front door together and stood there on the sidewalk a-looking up and down the street. There weren't no sign a' Cody nowhere.

"Did you search my—my wife's place yesterday?" Sly ast me.

"I never," I said, and I looked around at the other ones.

"It was on our path," said Miller, looking at Polly, "but we figured that Mr. Sly here was your friend, and we didn't need to—"

"Goddamn it, I said to search the whole damn town, didn't I?"

"Yes, sir, but—"

"Never mind that now," said Sly. "I'll take care of it." He started right across the street headed for the goddamned White Pigeon's Ass or whatever it was Miss Lillian called the prissy damn place. I told the rest where to go searching, and then I said to Bonnie, "Let's go back in and search our own damn place."

"All right," she said.

We turned around and walked back inside. The first thing we done was we walked real slow through the big main room and looked hard at ever'one in there. I kept a-thinking about what Sly had said about ole Cody changing the way he looked. But we knowed ever'one in the place. He weren't there. Bonnie headed for the stairway, but I stopped her. I walked behind the bar and went through the door what Aubrey went through to fetch breakfasts. It was a combination storeroom and kitchen, and me and Bonnie poked through it all, looking behind ever' stack a' boxes and into ever' corner. There weren't no one hiding in there.

We went back out and on over to the stairway. We started up the stairs kinder slow. About half-way up, I pulled out my Merwin and Hulbert, and I seed that Bonnie done the same thing. Whenever we got to the top a' the stairs, I walked over to the nearest door, what was the door to our own private room. Bonnie give me a kinder curious look, but I shooshed her, and I opened the door and stepped inside real quicklike and looked the room over real good. There wasn't no one in there. I stepped back out and pulled the door shut. Then I went on to the next door. I jerked that one open, and this time

Bonnie crowded in first. I stepped in behint her. We both looked over the room. It were empty. We went out and went on to the next one. The same thing.

We went about halfway down the hallway thatt-away, and I opened another door. A whore set up in bed and squealed. She had a cowboy in bed with her, from the night before, I reckoned. I told her to hush up and went back out in the hall. Me and ole Bonnie kept on a-going down the hallway. We found some more gals sleeping late on account a' their late-night work schedules. A couple of them never even woked up whenever we went into their rooms. But whenever we got to the last room, we still hadn't seed no sign a' no Cody. I opened up the outside door and stepped out onto the landing there and looked out onto the alley. There wasn't no one in the alley, and I couldn't see much a' the main street from where I was at. I did see a shiny democrat wagon pass by. I remember wondering who might be a-driving it, on account a' I couldn't recollect see-ing the damn thing before.

"Come on," I said to Bonnie, and I started down the stairs. Bonnie come waddling after me. I hol-stered my Merwin and Hulbert, and I guess Bonnie done the same thing. Then I headed for the street. First thing I done whenever I got to the street was to look after that damn democrat. I seed it parked down a ways about in front a' the gun shop, but I knowed, a' course, the gun shop was closed up. I started walking toward it.

"Barjack," said Bonnie, "ain't we going to check out these buildings?"

"Go on ahead if you want to," I said. "I'm check-ing something else first."

She stood there a minute kinder undecided-like, but then she come a-running after me. In another few minutes we had come to the democrat. It had one horse hitched to it, and it was just a-standing there. The door to the gun shop was still open from whenever we had kicked it open the day before, so I just pushed it and walked on in, pulling out my shooter on the way. It was kinder dark inside the place. It was still early morning. The sun weren't up very high yet. And a' course, there weren't no lamp lit. I squinnied my eyeballs and looked around. I didn't see no one. I walked back behint the counter and looked there, but I still didn't see no one. Bonnie come on in behint me, and then we checked the back room. It were empty.

"Damn it," I said.

I walked back out into the street with Bonnie hustling up right back a' me. I looked up and down the street. Then I looked right back in front a' me, and the damn thing was gone. "Where'd it go?" I said.

"What?" said Bonnie.

"The damn democrat wagon," I said. "It was right here whenever we went into the gun shop."

"Why, sure it was," she said. Then she went to looking up and down the street, almost kinder desperate. "I don't see it nowhere, Barjack."

I run out into the middle a' the street and hollered out as loud as I could for ole Butcher.

"Butcher, goddamn it. Butcher."

"Right here, Marshal."

I looked up and seed him standing on top of a roof right across the street.

"Butcher," I said, "did you see that goddamned democrat wagon come a-driving down the street?"

"That little one-horse job?" he said. "Painted black?"

"Yeah. That's the one."

"I seen it."

"Well, where the hell did it go?"

"It turned the corner right down yonder and disappeared," he said.

I think he just meant that he couldn't see it no more whenever it went around the corner, but I sure didn't like the word he chose to use in the saying of it. I run down there and around the corner. I didn't see no sign of it. I kept a-running till I come to the next corner, and then I looked up and down, and still I didn't see no sign of it. I thunk, how the hell could a man make a goddamned democrat wagon disappear just like that? I was breathing hard from that short run I made, and I turned around and walked a-huffing and puffing back to the main street. Bonnie come a-running to meet me.

"The son of a bitch is gone," I said. "It had to be Cody a-driving it. He's the only one I know who can make things disappear like that."

We walked back down to the gun shop, and then I seed Happy strolling along the street. I yelled at him, and he come over.

"Happy," I said, "I want you to go up on that roof over yonder and take Butcher's place. Tell him to come over here and see me."

"Yes, sir," he said, and he run off. In another few minutes Butcher come walking over to me.

"What is it, Barjack?" he said.

"Did you get a good look at whoever it was a-driving that democrat?" I ast him.

"I guess I got a fairly good look, but I didn't recognize him none."

"What'd he look like?"

"Well, I'd guess he was about Happy's size. I can't be sure. I was looking down on him, and he was sitting down driving the wagon. He was wearing a black suit and a black derby hat."

"Could you see his face atall?"

"Not real good, but I think it was smooth."

"No beard? No mustache?"

"I don't think so," Butcher said.

"Well, damn it all to hell," said Bonnie. "Sly was right."

Yeah, I thunk, Sly was right again. Cody was changing his appearance all right. I wondered what the son of a bitch would look like next time we seen him.

Chapter Seventeen

Well, I tuck me a stroll down to the stable and went on inside, and there was that goddamn democrat wagon just a-standing there in the middle a' the place. There wasn't no horse hitched to it no more. I seed the ole man what run the place, and I jumped him right off. "Where'd that damned thing come from just now?" I ast him.

"Feller rented it off a' me just returned it," he said.

"Just now?"

"Just a few minutes ago."

"Well, where'd he go?"

"How the hell would I know? He paid me my money, and he left. That's all."

"What did the son of a bitch look like?"

"He was wearing a black suit, and he had shaved off his mustache."

"Did he give you a name?"

"Jones is the name he give whenever rented the rig."

"Well, goddamn it, if you ever see him again, shoot the son of a bitch."

"Just shoot him?"

"You heared me. Shoot him dead. Then come

over to my office or to the Hooch House and tell me about it."

"Yes, sir, Marshal," he said, and I walked outta there and went on back to the Hooch House. Just as I was about to go inside, Butcher come up to me.

"What do you want me to do, Barjack?" he ast me.

"Keep a-looking," I said, and I went on inside and over to my table and set down. Aubrey brung me a tumbler full a' good whiskey.

"There's a man over at the bar looking for you," he tole me in a low voice. "He's looking for trouble, I think."

"Which one?" I ast.

"Fellow standing on this end," he said. "Wearing a brown vest."

I looked, and I seed the feller, but I didn't know his ass. "Tell him I'm here," I said.

"Yes, sir," said Aubrey, and he went back behind the bar. I watched outta the corner a' my eyeball, and I seed Aubrey lean across the bar and say something. The feller turned his head and looked at me. Then he picked up his drink and turned it down. I slipped my Merwin and Hulber self-extracting revolver outta the holster and helt it betwixt my legs underneath the table. Then I picked up my tumbler in my left hand. The stranger come a-walking toward me. Whenever he got close, he said, "Barjack?"

"That's right," I said. "Who's asking?"

"That ain't important," he said. "What's important is that a feller name a' Cody paid me to kill you."

His right hand mighta twitched, but then again,

it might notta. I didn't wait for nothing after he said what he done. I raised up the barrel a' my shooter and pulled the trigger, and my slug tore through the tabletop and ripped into his belly kindly low. I felt some bad about that. A low belly wound is right painful and not immediate deadly. He give a gasp and staggered back a couple a' steps. His right hand made like it was going for his gun, but it didn't seem to have no strength in it. I decided that he needed to be kilt right away on account a' he wasn't going to do nothing but suffer till he died nohow, so I brung my shooter up on top a' the table and fired again. This time I hit him in the heart, and he fell over back'ards deader'n hell.

Aubrey come out from behind the bar and walked over to stand by the carcass. "You kilt him, Barjack," he said.

"That was my intention," I said. "Search his pockets."

Aubrey dropped down on one knee and commenced to going through the dead guy's pockets. He come out with a watch and a jackknife and some pocket change. Then he said, "Well, looky here," and he went and tossed a wad a' bills up onto the table. I picked them up and counted five hundred dollars out. I wondered if that was how much he had been paid to kill me. "Hell," I said, "it damn sure weren't enough."

"What?" Aubrey said.

"The son of a bitch said he'd been paid to kill me," I tole him.

"Cody?" Aubrey said.

"Yup."

I picked up my drink and polished it off. Then I

helt the empty tumbler out toward Aubrey. He tuck it. "Fill this up for me," I said, "and then go out and find Butcher, and tell him to get his ass in here."

"But the bar won't be tended, Barjack," Aubrey said.

"Go on," I said. "I'll watch it."

So Aubrey brung my glass back all filled up, and then he tuck off. A cowhand got up from a table and staggered over to the bar. He banged his fist on the bar and hollered out. "Hey," he yelled. "I need a drink here. Right now."

"Hey you," I called out to him. "You at the bar."

He turned to look in my direction. "You talking to me?"

"Yeah. You."

"Well, what is it?"

"Cut out that goddamn caterwauling. Ole Aubrey will be back directly."

"But I want another drink."

"You can wait till Aubrey gets back."

"I said—"

Just then another cowpoke stepped up beside a' him and put a hand on his shoulder. He spoke to him kinder lowlike into the side a' his head, but I could hear what he was a-saying. "Take it easy, pard," he said. "That there's Barjack. You don't want to rile him."

"Barjack?" the first cowhand said.

"Yeah. Now come on back and set down and wait for Aubrey to get back. All right?"

"Yeah. Sure. I ain't in no hurry."

I seed the two a' them go back to the table and set down, and just about then Aubrey come back in. He fetched that poor cowboy his drink. Butcher come a-running in just then too, and he hurried on over to my table where I was a-setting.

"You want me, Barjack?" he ast, and then he seed that stiff a-laying there a-bleeding all over my floor with his eyes wide-open and looking up at the ceiling. "What's that?" he ast me.

"That's the reason I sent for you," I said. "I want you to get rid a' that. That damned Cody paid him to kill me. Leastwise, that's what he said before I blasted his ass."

"Cody paid him?" said Butcher.

"Yeah," I said, "and that likely means that he's paid some others as well, so we got to watch all the strangers what rides into town."

"Yes, sir," said Butcher. "You want me to haul this down to—"

"The boneyard," I said, finishing up his sentence for him.

Butcher leaned over the stiff and hauled him up and over his shoulder, and then he wobbled outta the place with his load on his back like a old packhorse. There was still a pool a' blood on the floor, but ole Aubrey had tuck note a' that, and he was out with a bucket a' water and a mop right quick after Butcher left, and he swabbed it up right quick and then went back behind the bar to tend to his duties.

Bonnie and Polly come in and set down with me. Bonnie waved at Aubrey, and he brung them each a drink. "Barjack," Bonnie said, "my ass is plumb wore out. We searched this whole damn town. Twice."

"And there ain't no sign of that goddamned Cody," Polly added.

"Well, the son of a bitch has been to the stable," I said. "He turned in that damned democrat wagon."

"You mean, since we seen it?" Bonnie said.

"Since we seed it," I said. "I went down to the stable, and there it set."

"Well, goddamn," Bonnie said, and she set up straight and looked around the room as if she might just spot him right in there in the Hooch House. Course she never.

"There's something else," I said.

"What?" Bonnie said.

"He's tuck to hiring men to kill me. I just kilt one of them right here a few minutes ago."

"And Cody hired him?" said Polly.

"That's what the man said just afore I shot him in the gut, and he had five hundred dollars on his ass."

"Where'd he get that kinda money?" said Polly.

"I'm damned if I know," I said, "but here it is," and I tossed it back out onto the table.

"What're you going to do with that?" Bonnie ast me.

"Stuff it down betwixt your sweet tits," I said. "It'll pay for the mess the bastard made in here. Hell, Aubrey had to mop up a whole damn pool a' blood off a' the floor. Right there."

The floor was still wet where the blood had been. Bonnie looked at it. Then she picked up the five hundred smackers and poked them down betwixt her tits, just like I told her.

"So there could be more," Polly said.

"That's the way I figgered it," I said. "Keep your eyes peeled for strangers toting guns."

"What do we do if we see a gun-toting stranger?" Bonnie said.

"Shoot them," I said.

A gunshot sounded outside, and much as I sure as hell didn't feel like it, I shoved back my chair and stood up. As I headed for the front door, Bonnie and Polly come after me. We got out on the sidewalk and seed ole Butcher standing there with his shooter in his hand and a poor wretch laying out in the street in a spreading pool a' blood with a big hole in his chest. He was wearing two guns, but they was both still in their holsters. I didn't know who the former person was.

"What the hell's going on here?" I said.

"I shot the son of a bitch, Marshal," said Butcher, "just like you said to."

I looked at Bonnie. "You know him?" I ast.

"I ain't never seen him before," she said.

"Me neither," I said. "I reckon he was a stranger all right. Check through his pockets, Butcher."

So Butcher went to digging, and guess what? He come up with five hundred bucks. I tole him to give it to Bonnie, and she put it with the rest. "Give me his guns," I said, and Butcher pulled off the belt and handed it to me. It was a nice, new-looking pair a' Smith & Westerns. Roosians, I think they was. Butcher looked up at me with a questioning look on his dumb face, and I said, "Take him off with the other'n." He did.

Me and the two gals went back inside, and it wasn't no time before ole Pisster-Peester, our pettifogging mayor, come hurrying in. He come right to my table and pulled out a chair and set down across from me a-staring straight into my face.

"What's the matter, Pisster?" I said. "You think I'm pretty to look at or what?"

"No, Barjack," he said, "I sure don't think you're pretty. In fact, I think you're one of the ugliest bastards I've ever looked at."

"Then how come you come in here to stare me in the face?"

"Barjack, what the hell is going on here?"

"We're just setting here having us a quiet drink," I said.

"I wouldn't call it quiet," he said. "Anything but quiet. You've had a small army out searching everything in town. And in the last few minutes, there've been two men killed. So what's going on?"

"Well, Mr. Mayorness," I said, "you know that son of a bitch Cody what robbed our bank and we got his whole gang but not him and we got the money back?"

"Yes. Of course."

"He's a-loose in town, and we're a-looking for him."

"How come you haven't found him?"

"On account a' he can make hisself invisible," I said.

"Oh, hell, that's not possible."

"Don't be too damn sure," I said. "You know, I learnt myself how to fly."

"I have heard that," the mayoralty said, "but I've never seen it."

"Do you have to see something to believe it?" I ast him.

"Most usually."

"Did you ever see the president of the United States?"

"No. I never have."

"Well, do you believe that there is such a thing?"

"Of course I do."

"So you see?"

"Oh, hell, Barjack, never mind about flight and invisibility. What about the two killings just a few minutes ago?"

"Cody hired them two assholes to kill me," I said. "I got one of them first, and Butcher got the other'n first."

"Are you sure of that?"

"Course I'm sure. They're both dead."

"No. I mean, are you sure that Cody hired them to kill you?"

"The first one tole me that he had just before I shot him dead, and then I found five hundred bucks on him. The second one had five hundred on him too."

Ole Pisster sure did look worried, and after all that converse, he looked like as if he didn't know what to say no more neither. Final he stood up and put the hat back on his head.

"All I can say is, hurry up and catch that Cody. We can't have a man like that running loose on our streets."

"We'll get the son of a bitch," I said. "I don't think he can stay invisible for too long at a time."

He give me a hell of a look then, and he hurried on outta the place.

Chapter Eighteen

Well, no one seen nothing a' that damned Cody for a couple a' days or more, I don't rightly recollect for exact. Me and ole Bonnie was setting, just the two of us, in the Hooch House at our own private table whenever she kindly invited me to go upstairs with her. I didn't have nothing else to do at the time, so I accepted, and we walked up the stairs and down the hallway to our private room. I was surprised on account a' she had a tub a' water waiting there. She had went and ordered it up without letting me know. The only thing was, it was plain, clear water. There weren't no suds in it nor nothing like for a regular bath.

Bonnie went to pulling the clothes off a' me, and whenever she had me stripped down nekkid, she tole me to get into the tub, and I done what she said. She peeled off her own things pretty damn quick too, and then she kindly startled me when she went and stepped over the edge a' the tub, getting one foot on either side a' me.

"Bonnie," I said. "Goddamn it. What the hell are you doing? There ain't room in here for the both of us."

"Oh, bullshit," she said. "There's a-plenty a' room."

Then she done it. She went and set down in the water, and whenever her mass went under the water, well, the water just natural rose up, and it rose up so high that it went and sloshed out all around. It sorter flooded the whole damn floor of our room. I was a-fixing to protest like hell, but she went and tuck a deep breath and ducked her head plumb down under the water, and what she done to me then, well, you wouldn't believe it if I was to tell you.

Now I thought I had seed it all, but that there really did take the cake. It was so damned exciting that I was finished in no time atall, and she come up outta the water with her mouth wide-open and gasping for air.

"Bonnie," I said, "where the hell did you learn how to do that? Damn, I thought you was about to drowned yourself down there."

"Did you like it, Barjack?" she said.

"Oh, hallelujah, sweet ass, I never even imagined nothing like it before in all my life."

Well, whenever we went back downstairs, Butcher and Happy was setting at my table, and it was all I could do to keep it to myself what had went on upstairs, but I knowed that Bonnie would knock the shit outta me if I said anything about it, so I kept my yap shut. Then Pisster come in and hurried over to my table.

"Barjack," he said.

"I can hear," I said, "you don't need to be a-yelling out into the street."

"All right," he said, quieting down his voice some,

and he pulled out a chair and set down. "All right, but he's been spotted again. He's still right here in town."

"You talking about that goddamned Cody bastard?" I said.

"That's just who it is I'm talking about," he said. "Your Indian friend spotted him just as he went around the corner. He chased him, but he never saw him again."

"You sure about that?" I said.

"I heard it right straight from the Indian," he said.

"You still gonna tell me that it's impossible for him to make hisself invisible?" I ast him.

"Oh, hell," he said, "I don't know anything about that."

"Where's Miller at now?" I said.

"Still looking, I guess," Pisster said.

"Come on," I said to Butcher and Happy, "let's go give him a hand."

They followed me out, and so did Bonnie, even though I weren't really talking to her whenever I said that. We done the whole thing over again, what we had already did several times. We went from building to building. Me and Bonnie wound up back at Widder Rogers's place, and even though the widder was still setting in jail, we went inside. Whenever we barged into the room that Cody had rented under the name a' Jones, a man what was laying on the bed jumped up surprised.

"What's the meaning of this?" he said.

"Who the hell are you," I said, "and what the hell are you a-doing in here?"

"I rented this room legitimately," he said. "What right have you to barge in here this way?"

"He's got every right. He's Marshal Barjack," Bonnie said. She was holding her little Merwin and Hulbert .38 out in front a' herself.

"Marshal?" the man said. He was of a average height and weight, and he was dressed up kindly like a miner. He had a red beard and a headful a' red hair. I couldn't recall that I had ever seed him before nowhere.

"Now that we got that all straight," I said, "let's set down and you answer me a few questions."

"Sure thing, Marshal," he said, and he set on the edge a' the bed.

"How can you have rented this place legitimate," I said, "when I have got the owner locked up in my jailhouse? And when I locked her up, this here room was rented out to someone else?"

"Oh. Well, I rented it from a man named Jones," he said. "He told me he could sublet it."

Me and Bonnie give each other a look.

"What's your name?" I asked the feller.

"Pennybaker," he said. "Did I do something wrong?"

"I reckon not," I tole him, "but if you see that Jones again, come by my office or the Hooch House and let me know. Right away."

"Yes, sir," he said. "I'll do that."

Well, the search ended up that night just like it had them other times, except that night, I set out sentries on all a' the ways outta town. I got ole Pisster to back me up on that, so we knowed that we had Cody hemmed up in town. There wasn't no way for him to get out. Course that hadn't never been our problem. Our problem was that we knowed he was in town, and we still couldn't find the chickenshit son of a bitch. He disappeared. Never mind what that damned pettifogging mayor had said. Cody disappeared whenever he wanted to. We decided to try another tactic this time. I had Happy and Butcher ride down the street and yell for ever'one to get outside and stand in the street. Then Miller and Polly and me and Bonnie checked inside the buildings. We done that with ever' street in the whole damn town. We never found him.

I begun to wonder what a invisible man et, on account a' we couldn't find no one in town what had fed him or seed him eat a meal nowhere. Anyhow, a couple a' nights later, me and Bonnie was in the Hooch House again and there weren't no one left in there but 'cept me and her. Ever'one else was out watching the streets. She give me a coy invite up to our private room, suggesting that we might repeat the wonderful adventure what we'd had the last time. I went up with her in a hurry, and pretty soon we had a tub a' warm, clean water setting in the middle a' the room. I got nekkid and clumb in, and Bonnie done the same thing as she had did the last time, even to sloshing out half a' the water. Then she sucked in a lungful a' air and went under. She was hard at work under there, whenever the door of our room come open, and that redheaded and red-bearded feller from the widder's house stepped inside and looked at us.

"Goddamn it," I yelled. "What the hell are you a-doing here?" I didn't figger he was just returning the favor of a unannounced visit.

Well, I reckon that sound a' my voice carried

right on under the water, on account a' Bonnie heared it and come up and looked over her shoulder and seed that damned Pennybaker a-standing there. She let out a hell of a shriek and stood up, but whenever she stood, her feet went and slipped on the slick bottom a' the tub, and she fell over back'ards, but only she never fell plumb outta the tub. Instead, her great big butt landed on the back edge a' the tub, and her massive weight went and caused that end a' the tub to go over and land on the floor, and the other end a' the tub to rise up. Whenever that happened, a' course, all a' the water was slung out and all over Pennybaker, and Bonnie went sliding across the floor. She stopped when she run into Pennybaker's feet. I come outta that tub too, flying out face-first, and my head went sliding up betwixt Bonnie's legs.

Pennybaker slipped too; whenever Bonnie run into his legs, his feet went to slipping on the wet floor, and he landed on his ass right in the middle a' the open doorway. When his butt hit the floor, he fired a shot into the ceiling. I commenced to scampering across the floor on my hands and knees toward my gun as fast as ever I could go, and he was a-trying to get back up on his feet, but he was still a-sliding. I made it to my Merwin and Hulbert and pulled it out and turned it on the son of a bitch. He was just about up on his feet again, and before I could shoot, I seed that his red hair was nothing but a damned moppy-looking wig, and the water sloshing on him had knocked it kindly cockeyed.

"Cody," I said, "you son of a bitch," and I snapped off a shot, but just as I did, he slipped again and fell back onto his ass. My shot went high over his head, and he turned and scooted out the door. I managed to get up onto my own two bare feet, but when I went to walking, I slipped on the wet floor and went back down again. "Goddamn it," I yelled. I got up again, and this time I walked kindly like a penguin so I wouldn't slip again. I had to step across ole Bonnie's big shape, and I did final get my bare nekkid ass out in the hallway, and I looked up and down but I never seed the son of a bitch nowhere. He coulda gone either way.

I hurried on down to the far end a' the hall and stepped out onto the outside landing. I never seed him, but a woman passing by seed me and shrieked. "To hell with you," I shouted at her, and I went back inside and hurried to the other end a' the hall, where the landing overlooked the saloon. I was standing on the very spot from where ole Bonnie had flung my ass that time I had learnt to fly. "Hey," I shouted. "Anyone see a red-haired bastard come down these stairs after them shots was fired?" Well, ever'one in the whole damned place looked up whenever I shouted out like that, and a' course, they all seed me standing there nekkid as a goddamned owl and holding my shooter ready. I 'spect they was all a-wanting to laugh at me, but they was skeered to. Several said no and shuck their heads. The son of a bitch had disappeared on me once again.

I plopped my goddamned bare feet back into the room and set my ass back down on the bed. I was plumb by God pissed off. I was getting goddamned tired of that disappearing bastard. I wanted him to stand up and face me like a real man, and I begun to get a idee a' how Miller the Churkee and ole Pistol

Polly was a-feeling about him. They had more reason to hate his guts than what I had, and then they had the same reasons on top a' all that as what I had.

I reached over to the table for the bottle a' whiskey what we kept in our room, and I found it near empty. I picked up the glass from off the table anyhow and poured the remains a' that bottle in it. Bonnie had final managed to get her ass up of a' the wet floor, and she waddled over to the bed. "Barjack," she said, "did he—"

"The son of a bitch disappeared again," I said. "He's still a-loose in our streets."

"You want me to fetch you your clothes?" she ast me.

"No," I said, "hell, I'm too pissed off to get dressed. I'm just going to set here nekkid and get drunk."

"I'll get something on," she said, "and go get you a fresh bottle."

"That'd be real nice, pussy willow," I said.

She shrugged herself into something and left the room, and I set there getting more and more pissed off. The whole damn room was wet. The bath tub was standing on its goddamn end, and I was setting there nekkid and wet too a-holding on to my Merwin and Hulbert self-extracting revolver a-thinking about killing a feller name a Cody. When Bonnie come back to the room with the bottle, I tuck it and opened it and poured me a whole damn glassful.

"Aubrey asked me what the hell we was up to up here," she said. "Water's leaking through the roof down behind the bar. He even got his head dripped on, and he was pouring a glass a' whiskey for a man, and water come running down in it."

"Tell Aubrey to charge a little less for watered whiskey," I told her, "and tell him that anything further about the water ain't none a' his goddamned business."

"I'll tell him," she said.

Then I ast her to go out and find my depitties and send one to each end a' our landing to watch out for that bastard Cody. She hustled her ass off to do that, and I tuck me a long, long drink.

That Cody had me so frustrated that I commenced to wondering if maybe ole Pisster was right about me being over the hill. I knowed I was a-getting older, but I hadn't never thunk much about that. I went to thinking about it just then, though. I thunk about that time me and Miller and Polly had been set afoot in the hills, and I like to've died trying to keep up with them two young'uns. And I thunk about that Cody what kept disappearing on me. Course, he kept disappearing on ever'one else too, but I never considered that. I was feeling sorry for my own ass. I wondered if I did get the bastard right smack in front a' my eyeballs if I would be fast and accurate enough to take him out.

Now, I hadn't never worried about shit like that before. I would ruther have just slipped up behind a damned owl hoot and shot him in the back or maybe bashed him over the head, but that son of a bitch had me squirrely. Even though I had learnt to fly, a man disappearing on me like he was a-doing was enough to get me kinder shuck up. I thunk about maybe retiring, if we ever was to get Cody. Then I thunk about Cody maybe retiring me unvoluntary, if you get my meaning. Retiring me from ever'thing. For good. I didn't like that thought too damn good.

I caught myself thinking that I hoped that Miller would run up against him before I had to, or even Pistol Polly. I imagined either one a' them blasting Cody straight to hell, and then I had a kinda vision a' Polly and Miller both a-blasting away at Cody, but just before their bullets shoulda tore into him, the bastard just disappeared. Goddamn but I was a mess. I looked at my glass and seed that I had drunk it empty, so I got the bottle and poured my glass back full again. I dranked that glass off in a hurry too. I wondered what ole Dingle would think about me getting too old. Would he ever write another book about ole Barjack?

I got to wondering what he would call his next book. *Barjack, Over the Hill*, or maybe *Barjack Grows Old* or *Barjack's All Washed Up*. I damn near laughed out loud, and I thunk that I would maybe suggest them there titles to the scribbler my own self. I tuck another drink, and then I said out loud but really to no one but my own self, "No, I ain't neither. I ain't washed up, and I ain't too old. I'll show them all, including that damned pettifogger and the scribbler. I'll get that goddamned murdering bastard myself with my Merwin and Hulbert. Or maybe I'll begin to toting a shotgun along with me wherever I go. I'd like to see the son of a bitch disappear on a shotgun. It'd damn sure leave a visible blood smear where he had used to be."

I dranked down the second glass a' whiskey and poured me a third, and then Bonnie come back into the room. "Happy's down yonder at the outdoor landing," she said, "and Butcher's down here at the other end."

"Good," I said. "Now you come here to me." I had

done talked myself into feeling better by then, and I grabbed Bonnie by her fat arm and pulled her onto the bed with me. "You and me has got some unfinished business together."

"Oh, Barjack," she said.

Chapter Nineteen

Now, I'm here to tell you that things changed considerable around Asininity about that time. That son of a bitch Cody had got us all as nervous as a cottontail rabbit looking straight into a whole passel a' hungry coyotes. For the next week ever'one seed Cody somewhere or nother. But he disappeared right after he was saw. It got to where I was expecting to see the bastard around ever' corner I come to. And I damn sure do believe that Bonnie and Miller and Polly and Dingle and both a' my depitties was all the same way. The onliest one what weren't acting thattaway was ole Sly the Widdamaker. Nothing in the world seemed to be able to ruffle him one goddamned bit. I tell you, I never seed no one as cool as Sly. Not in my whole life.

I was a-setting in my marshaling office in the middle a' one afternoon. I didn't really have no reason to be in there. I just wanted to assert my ass some, I guess, let ever'one know I was still the law in town, and ole Happy, he was a-setting in there too. I didn't say nothing about Happy just setting around on account a' to tell you the whole and plain truth, I was glad to have some company. I had just tuck out my bottle a' stash from my desk drawer and was a-reaching for two glasses when the door come a-flying open. My hand went straight to my Merwin and Hulbert, and Happy, what was a-setting with his back to the door, jumped up and hauled out his Colt. But it wasn't no Cody.

It was ole Butcher what come in, and he was a-staggering and holding his head, and his head was bloody too. He looked around and spied a chair setting against one a' the walls, and staggered over to it and dropped down in a setting position. He moaned right out loud.

"Butcher," Happy said, putting away his Colt.

I come out from behint my desk and headed for him. "What the hell happened?" I ast him.

"I was walking down this way from the Hooch House," Butcher said, "and I walked by that space between two buildings down there, you know, and someone hit me on the head. I guess he come outta that dark space. He hit me hard, and I went down. I think I was knocked out for a spell. I don't know how fucking long. Anyhow, when I come around, I got up and headed down here."

"Did you get a look at him?" Happy ast.

"I never," Butcher said, "but it was that goddamn Cody."

"How do you know that?" I ast.

"Who the hell else could it a' been?"

"Happy," I said, "walk Butcher over to the doc's, and then fetch the Widdamaker and send him over here."

"Yes, sir," said Happy. He helped Butcher to stand up, and he steadied him whilst he walked, and they went outta the office and headed for Doc's. I set back down behint my desk and pulled out my six-gun and laid it on the desk in front a' me. I thunk about it for a minute. Then I jumped up and went over to the gun rack and got me a shotgun. I made sure it was loaded, and I put it on my desk. Then I set back down and got me a glass outta the drawer and poured me a good drink a' whiskey. I drunk it all down almost at one gulp. Then I poured another one.

I was about halfway through that second drink when ole Sly come a-walking in. "What is it, Barjack?" he said.

"Did Happy fetch you?" I said.

"Yes, he did."

"Did he tell you what happened to ole Butcher?"

"He said that Butcher got knocked on the head pretty bad."

"That's right. Just down the street here and in the middle a' the goddamn day. It was most likely that son of a bitch Cody. I want you to walk down there with me and check it out."

"All right," he said.

I stood up and finished off my drink. Then I put my Merwin and Hulbert back into my holster and picked up the shotgun. I headed for the door, but Sly had beat me to it. He opened it up and stepped aside for me. I went out and he followed and closed the door. Then we walked side by side down the street to the spot what Butcher had told me about. I seed a little blood on the sidewalk, I reckoned where ole Butcher had fell down. Poking the shotgun in ahead a' me, I stepped into the dark space. Sly follered me with a Colt in his hand. I squinnied my eyeballs at the dark, but I never seed no one in there.

Then at the far end a' the space there right by the

alley, a figger in a long black coat stepped out into the space just long enough to hurry around the corner and disappear. Before I had time to think about it, I raised up the shotgun and fired off a blast. I felt like a damned greenhorn, wasting a shot like that. "Damn it," I said.

Sly squeezed past me and went to running after the bastard. I tuck out after him. He was around the corner in a hurry. It tuck me a little longer, but whenever I come out in the alley, I seed Sly down a couple a' buildings and rounding another corner. I went after him as fast as I could, but my old legs just wouldn't work none too good no more. I heared a shot. When I final went around that corner, Sly was a-standing there with his Colt in his hand.

"Did you get him?" I said.

"I don't think so," he said. "I think I hit the long tail of that cloak he's wearing."

"Where'd he go?" I ast.

"Barjack," Sly said, "you're not likely to believe this, but when I shot, it was almost like he just disappeared. I have no idea which way he turned."

"I believe it," I said. "I been hearing stories like that for two weeks now. Well, let's walk over there and take a look."

We walked down to the end a' the building, what was the front, and we was back out on the main street. We looked both ways, and we didn't see no one what looked nothing like Cody, but Sly leaned over to pick up a black cloak. He helt it up by one a' the corners, and I seed his bullet hole.

"No way that hit him," he said.

"Where the hell could he a' gone?" I said out loud but not really asking Sly, just talking.

We was a-standing in front a' the big winder at the front a' Augie the saddle maker's shop. Augie was inside a-working on a set a' harness. Sly opened the door and stepped inside. Holding up the long black cloak, he said, "Did you see the man that dropped this?"

"Yeah," Augie said.

"Which way did he go?"

"He looked to me like he was headed for the Hooch House," Augie said.

"Let's go," I said, and me and Sly moved on down the sidewalk. Back behint us I heared Augie call out, "Say, Marshal, what'd he do?"

As we was a-moving along, I seed Happy and Dingle acrost the street, and up ahead of us I seed the Churkee and Polly moving in the opposite direction from us a-headed for the Hooch House too. They was a whole bunch a' folks out on the sidewalk and in the street, and to this day I don't know how come, but the street was sure enough crowded that day, I can tell you that. Then all of a sudden-like, we all heared a booming and fearful-sounding voice come down like from the clouds.

"You fine-haired sons of bitches," it roared, "I'll kill you all."

I reckon all of us in town went and looked up to see if we could see God's face in the sky, but what we did see was Cody hisself. He was standing on the peak a' the bank's facade. It were the highest place he could get on main street. He was holding a six gun in each hand, and of a sudden, he went to shooting. He dropped a cowboy in the middle a' the street. A whole bunch of folks went diving for cover. One man went headlong into a watering trough, and he went clean under the water. I don't know how he was a-breathing. I yelled out in general, "Get the son of a bitch."

It seemed like ever'one on the street went to shooting, me included, and I could see the bullets a-hitting in that facade, kicking up splinters around Cody's feet, but it didn't seem like none of them ever did hit him. Then there come so many bullets around him that I couldn't see how some of them didn't get him, and maybe some did, on account a' he yelled out loud like a stuck pig, and you could hear him yell over the noise of all them shots, and he fell over back'ards, and I heared a loud crash.

"Surround the bank," I called out, and men with guns went to running toward the bank, some to the sides and some around to the back side. I went to the back. "Anyone see him come down off a' there?" I ast.

"Nope," said one a' the men back there.

"How the hell'd he get his ass up there?" I ast.

Happy was over to my left near the corner a' the building, and he said, "There's a ladder over on this side, Barjack."

"Well, climb your ass up there and take a look," I said, "but be careful when you get to the top that he don't plug you in the head."

"Yes, sir," Happy said, and he went around the corner. I follered to watch him. I was a-thinking as he started up that there ladder what a fool thing that was to do. If someone had tole me to do that, I'da tole him to go suck on a raw egg, a buzzard's egg for that, but ole Happy, he always done what I tole him to do. He was a good kid and a damn good depitty. He was about halfway up that long ladder, and I had my shooter out and was a-watching that roof for any sign a' Cody. I never seed none.

Happy got up where he could peek over the roof, and he called down, "He ain't up here, Barjack."

"He's got to be up there, the son of a bitch," I yelled.

"Well, he ain't." Ole Happy went on up over the edge, and he walked out onto the roof, where I lost sight of him. Ever' one waited real anxious. Then Happy called out again. "Barjack," he said, "there's a big hole in the roof."

"What?"

"There's a big hole in the roof. You know, when we seed him fall and we heared that crash? Well, I think he fell right through the roof."

"Well, I be goddamned," I said. "You stay where you're at, Happy, and the rest a' you stay where you are too. I started around the building, and I picked up Butcher on the side. Out front I found Sly, and I tuck them two with me into the bank by way a' the front door. Ever'thing looked normal. One a' the tellers seed me, and he come walking over to me.

"Can I help you, Marshal?" he ast me.

I was a-looking up at the ceiling, but I never seed no hole. "Yeah," I said, "I want you to take me into ever'room in this here building."

"Now?"

"Right now, goddamn it."

Well, he did. He tuck me into the president's office and the back room and ever'where, and I looked up at the ceiling in all a' them places. There wasn't no hole. I grumbled and went outside. I walked around to the ladder and climbed up and onto the damned roof. My idea was to throw Happy off, but instead I walked over to the peak a' the facade, and by God, there was the hole in the roof right where Happy had said it was. I pushed back my hat to scratch my head. This was a puzzle.

"Happy," I said, "I come up here to throw you off the roof for lying to me, but you ain't lied. There it is, by God."

He give me a kinda stupid look, like he didn't have no idea what the hell I was a-talking about, and I reckon he didn't neither, so I tole him. "I went all through that bank, ever'room, and there ain't no hole nowhere inside."

"Then he's in there," Happy said.

"In where?"

"He's between the roof and the ceiling," Happy said. "He's got to be."

"By God, you're right," I said. I walked over to the edge and hollered at Butcher and Sly to come on up. They did, but so did Miller and Polly. I showed them the hole, and I told them what I had found inside the bank and what Happy had said. "So now, what do we do?"

Butcher said, "Well, we could stay up here and all around the bank till he starves to death."

"I ain't so sure I want to hang around on the roof here for that long," I said.

"One or two of us could go down that hole and look for him," said Miller.

"The problem with that is that soon as you showed your ass down that hole, Cody'd be apt to blast it," I said.

"Let's get everyone out of the bank," said Sly. "Then we'll walk over this whole roof and shoot down into it. One of us is bound to get him."

"That's a good idee," I said, and I sent Happy down to clear the bank out. He was back real soon and said it was did, and so we all pulled out our guns and went to shooting down. We walked all over that roof and peppered it with bullets. There wasn't no way nobody coulda lived through that.

"Happy," I said, "go down in there now."

"Yes, sir," he said, and he walked over to the hole in the roof and eased himself down into it. Butcher come along behind him and said, "Me too," and he follered Happy right down into that there potential trap. I kept waiting to hear a gunshot, but I never. Happy come a-crawling back over to the hole, and he looked up. "Barjack," he said, "you got any matches?"

"What for?" I said.

"It's dark in here."

I reached into my pocket and pulled out a few and dropped them down into his hat, and he crawled off somewhere again. By an' by, he come back, Butcher with him, and they come up outta the hole. Both of them was shaking they heads.

"He ain't there," said Happy.

"Nowhere," said Butcher.

"You come across any blood?" I ast.

"No, sir," said Happy, and Butcher was shaking his head.

I looked at Sly. "This don't make a bit a' sense," I said. "Not a goddamn bit."

"Maybe he's a ghost," Polly said. I wanted to say that was about a stupid thing to say, but before I could say it, I caught myself thinking that maybe she was right, maybe we had done kilt him, and he was a-haunting us for it. The way things had been going, that was about the only thing that made any sense atall. He was a goddamned ghost.

"No," said Miller, "I don't think so."

"No?" said Polly. "How come?"

"Well, for starters," he said, "a ghost would have just slid right through that roof. It wouldn't have crashed through like that."

"What do you mean?" she said.

"A ghost can walk right through a brick wall without even displacing one brick," he said.

"How the hell do you know that? Have you ever seen a goddamn ghost?"

Chapter Twenty

Well, now, I kinda thunk that Miller was right in what he said about ghosts, but then what Polly said kinda set me to thinking that she might be right too. Hell, I hadn't never seed no ghost. I couldn't rightly say that he could go through a wall or a ceiling or whatever without smashing it. Miller said he wouldn't smash it, but damned if I knowed the truth a' the matter. For all that, hell, I didn't even know if there was any such thing as a goddamn ghost, and I sure as hell didn't want to find out for certain.

"I know, Barjack," said Happy.

"Aw," I said, "what the hell do you know?"

"Whenever he fell through the rooftop, he was alive, so he crashed through it, but then he died, and so he just slud through the ceiling without crashing it or nothing. Or maybe he slud back through the roof. Why, hellfire, if he's a ghost he might could be standing right here amongst us right now, and we not even know it on account a' we can't see a ghost."

"All right, smart-ass," I said, "what the hell kilt him after he went and crashed through the roof? Landing on the upper side a' the ceiling?"

"Well, maybe one of us shot him."

I couldn't answer that one. Maybe we had shot the son of a bitch and kilt him. We damn sure ventilated that rooftop a-trying. I sure didn't have no other explanation for his damned disappearing thattaway. But I still never wanted to believe we was a-dealing with a dead ghost now.

"Let's get down off a' this son of a bitch," I said.

We all of us clumb on back down, and I went back inside a' the bank, and ever'one follered me in there. We walked all through that damned bank, ever' room in the whole building including the presidunt's office. There wasn't no sign that ole Cody nor any other stranger had been in there atall, and they damn sure weren't no holes in the damned ceiling nowhere. I told Happy to stay in the bank just in case anything was to happen there, and I tole Butcher to go back up on the roof and keep his eyes open wide. I headed back for the Hooch House, and Miller and ole Sly walked along with me. I don't know what the rest of them did.

We was about to go inside whenever we heared a shot, and it sounded like as if it had come from the bank, where we had just come from. "The bank, Barjack," said Sly, and we all of us turned around to run back there, and whenever we turned, we seed that son of a bitch in his long-tailed black coat a-running down the street with a gun still in his hand. He went around the first corner he come to. We went hauling ass after him.

But I swear to God, he went and disappeared again. We went around the same corner what he had went around, and we opened ever'door we come to and looked inside. We walked the whole way down the alley doing the same thing, but it just weren't no use. He had really disappeared. I looked at ole Sly. "Widdamaker," I said, "do a ghost shoot a gun?"

"I wouldn't think so, Barjack," he said, "but if a man saw a ghost, he might shoot at it."

"Happy?" I said.

"Happy sure thinks we're dealing with a ghost," Sly said.

I felt a bit a' panic then, and I started to run again back toward the bank. "Happy's in the bank," I yelled. Sly run ahead a' me, and I like to died before we got back to the bank. There wasn't no one in the bank yet again 'cept for ole Moneybags whut I called him, the boss banker, you know, and when I final got there and run inside. Sly was kneeling down beside a Happy what was laid out like as if he was kilt. Moneybags was standing off to one side looking worried as all hell. I felt like crying. I mean it. I walked over there and got down beside ole Sly, and then I seed that a bullet had dug a bad crease along the right side a' Happy's head just at the right level where it cut his right ear plumb in half whenever it got that far along. "He ain't dead, is he?" I kinda choked out.

"He's alive," Sly said, "and I think he'll be all right, but we'd better get him to the doctor right away."

"Yeah," I said. "Let's haul him on over there."

So me and ole Sly picked up Happy, and I never knowed his ole skinny ass could be so damn heavy, but I never complained none, even though I was still wore out from that running what I done. Doc said Happy would be all right, and that made me feel some better, even though Sly had already said it. Well, we left Happy there in good hands and went back to the bank. Moneybags come a-running at me.

"Barjack," he said, "we've been robbed."

"The bastard what shot Happy?" I said.

"Yes."

"Tell me about it," I said.

"Well, I went to open up the vault to put today's money away. After what had already happened I was a bit nervous, you can understand. He was in there. In the vault. He pointed a gun at me, and I held up my hands and said something like don't shoot, and just then Happy said put up your hands, mister. You're under arrest, and the man shot Happy and ran outside."

Me and ole Sly, we looked at each other, and we both said at the same time, "In the vault," and we rushed over to the vault what was still open and stepped in it and looked up, and sure enough there was a hole in the damn ceiling up there. Cody had fell plumb through. We had just failed to look inside the vault.

"So it weren't no ghost," I said.

"No," Sly said, "but he still disappeared again. I'd call him ghostlike."

I set Moneybags to counting his cash so's he could let me know how much had been got away with, and then I went back to the Hooch House, after I called Butcher down off the roof, and Sly went back to Lillian's place. I found Bonnie and Polly and Miller and Dingle all in there, and then me and Butcher set our ass down too. Then someone said where's Happy, and I had to tell them all the whole story.

"When Cody fell through the roof," Polly said, "he fell through the ceiling right into the damn vault. That's just like the son of a bitch."

"Yeah, and then he went and disappeared again," I said. "Sly called him ghostlike."

Dingle was a-scribbling. I figgered he was for sure writing down that ghostlike.

"But Happy's gonna be all right?" Bonnie ast, sounding a little bit worried.

"He's just going to be a mite uglier than usual," I said. "He'll have a fine scar right acrost the right side a' his face, and his right ear is tore plumb in half. Other than that he'll be just fine."

She punched me on the shoulder hard enough to rock my chair up on two legs and skeer me I might turn over, and at the same time she shouted at me, "Barjack!"

Just about then Aubrey showed up with my glass a' whiskey and a drink for Butcher. Ever'one else seemed to be doing all right. Bonnie shoved her chair back and stood up.

"I'm a-going over to Doc's," she said, "and see Happy."

"I'll go with you," said Polly, and the two gals left the place, leaving just me and Butcher and Miller the Churkee and Dingle the scribbler. We wasn't very good company, not even for each other, and by and by ole Miller he said, "Barjack, shouldn't we be out hunting for that damn Cody?"

"Churkee," I said, "you do whatever the hell it is you want to do. Right now I don't even want to be thinking about no ghostlike son of a bitch, much less be out a-chasing after him."

Well, he finished his drink and left. Butcher kinda

sheepish said, "Barjack, should I ought to go along with him?"

"Not 'less you want to," I said. "I never sent him out. I don't like to send folks out on wild-goose chases like that."

"Well then," he said. "I guess I'll just stay here."

"Good. I need some company 'sides ole Dingle there. He don't even look up from his scribbling. He's worse than no company atall."

"I'm not that bad," said Dingle, but he never even looked up from his scribbling.

Right then in walked a bastard a-wearing a long-tailed black coat, and he walked right up to the bar and ordered a whiskey. I put my hand on my Merwin and Hulbert and kinda stiffened up somewhat. It come into my head that I could stand up and go after him and then he would just disappear. I didn't think I could stand that. In another minute Sly come in. He stopped just inside the door and looked hard at that man in the black coat. Then he looked over at me kinda puzzledlike. He walked over to my table and sat down acrost from me. He nodded toward the black coat.

"Is that him?" he ast me.

"I don't know," I said. Hell, all I could see was that long-tailed black coat. And just then another one come in. He walked to the far end a' the bar and ordered hisself a whiskey. Neither one a' them two bastards looked at me or at Sly, nor for that matter at each other, and I thought that was a little peculiar for two men looking like twins to show up in the same saloon and not even notice each other. Sly looked at me again, but then right quick I seed him look toward the door. I twisted

my head, and I seed two more black-coated bastards come a-walking in and not paying no notice
to one another nor to the first two what was already in there. They both walked up the bar and
ordered whiskey, but whenever they got their drinks,
one of them went to a table at one a' the front corners a' the place and the last one, number four,
I'll call him, I guess, he went to the other front
corner.

"What is this, Barjack?" Sly said. Dingle were
a-scribbling as fast as he could. "Hell if I know," I
said.

"You think we can take the four of them?" Sly
said.

"They's pretty damn scattered out," I said.

"That's what's worrying me."

"I'll take the one at the far end a' the bar," said
Butcher. We was all talking in real low tones. Then
I seed Dingle slip a hand in his coat pocket, and I
knowed that he had that there British Webley in
his pocket. "I'm with you," he said. "I'll take that
closest one."

"That just leaves you and me, Barjack," said
Sly. "Which one do you want?"

"The bastard on this side a' the room," I said,
and I was asking myself what the hell should I do?
Should I try to arrest them and haul their ass to
jail? Or should I just yell shoot and kill all four of
the sons a' bitches? They was all dressed like that
damned Cody, and it were obviously some kinda
setup, likely just to get me nervous as all get out,
and it were working kinda. But then I decided that
I really would like to get at least one a' them alive.
"Butcher," I said, "go on over and see can you ar-

rest yours. We'll cover you. Boys, keep your eyes on your own target. Go on now, Butcher."

"Sure thing, boss," he said, and he stood up and walked over to his man at the bar. He tapped the man on the shoulder. The man turned to look at him. Butcher said something and the man responded. Butcher said something else and hauled out his gun. The man backed up some, surprised-like, and he kinda raised up his both hands some. Then he walked outta the Hooch House in front a' Butcher. I never seed Butcher take no gun from the son of a bitch, though. I never thought that he were that damn dumb. "Dingle," I said, "you think you can do that?"

"It looks pretty simple, Barjack," he said, and he stood up and hitched his britches and stuck the Bulldog pistol in his pocket again but kept his hand in there with it. He walked to the bar and stepped up right behind and right close to his man. He reached out with his free hand and tapped the man on the shoulder. The man turned around.

"What?" he said. "What is it?"

"I'm a deputy town marshal," said Dingle.

"Is that supposed to bother me?" the man said. We could hear these two on account they was a whole lot closter to us than the first two.

"I'm placing you under arrest."

"What the hell for?"

"You can take that up with the marshal later." Dingle slipped the Bulldog out of his pocket and pointed the business end of it at the man.

"Hey," the man said. "You're serious."

"Damn right I'm serious," said Dingle. "Now get to marching." He nodded his head toward the front door, and the man started walking. They went right through the door and on outside. Me and ole Sly give each other a look.

"Me next?" Sly ast.

"Go on ahead," I said, and he stood up. He walked to the far front corner a' the room, and pretty soon I seed him walking that feller out the front door. I couldn't hear nothing neither one a' them said, but it sure didn't take hardly no time atall. Well, it were comed down to me then. I couldn't think a' no way to put it off no longer. I weren't skeered a' the bastard. Hell, his three look-alikes had gone and let theyselfs be marched off to jail without even much of a fuss. I were thinking that when I got to the jail with this bastard, there wouldn't be no one in my jail cells. They would all have disappeared.

Well, I still had a good gulp a' whiskey in my tumbler, so I picked it up and turned it down. Damn, but that were good whiskey. I stood up. "See you, Barjack," Aubrey kinda called out to me. I waved at him and headed for the front door, but before I reached it, I turned real sharp to my left and walked over to that feller there in the long-tailed black coat. When he seed that I was a-coming at him, he looked up and he kindly smiled.

"Hi, there," he said. "Looking for a place to sit down?"

"No," I said, pulling out my Merwin and Hulbert and pointing it at him. "I'm fixing to take you outta here and over to the jailhouse."

"Wha-wha-what for?" he stammered.

"You'll find out in due time," I said.

"Will you let me finish my drink?" he said. I looked at it and he did have a good swaller left. I hated to deprive a man of a good drink, especial when he has done paid for it.

"Go on ahead and drink it," I said, and he did in one fast gulp. Then he stood up. "Let me have your gun," I said.

"I—I don't have one," he said.

"Hold that there coat wide open," I said, and he pulled it open. I patted him down real cautiouslike, and by God, he hadn't lied to me. He weren't packing no gun. I gestured him toward the front dore and he started walking. I pointed in the right direction whenever we got on the sidewalk. As we was walking down he street, me behint him with my shooter out, I was thinking about the ghostlike Cody and now his four look-alikes and wondering what I was going to find in my jail. We got there final and stepped inside and Sly and Dingle and Butcher was all there, and they was three long black-coated shitheads a-setting my jail cell and looking downright puzzled and pissed off at the same damn time.

"Put this one in, Butcher," I said, and he did. Then I said, "Take that one what you arrested and take him in the back room and question him some. I want to know do he know Cody, and I want to know how come him to be dressed like he is and to be in my saloon right when he was."

"I'll find out for you, boss," Butcher said, and he grinned real big and tuck the first black coat outta the cell and into the back room. The other three were looking after them and looking worried.

"Don't worry, fellers," I said. "He'll get around to you by and by. Just then we heared a loud smack from outta the back room.

Chapter Twenty-one

Well, by God, Butcher come dragging that ole boy back out right away after that smack what we heared and put him back in the cell with the other'ns. Then he turned back to look at me, and he was a-grinning. "So?" I said to him.

"He said a feller what was dressed like he is now paid him ten smackers to put on them clothes and go into the Hooch House and have a couple a' drinks," Butcher said.

"Is that all?" sez me.

Butcher's smile faded off, and he said, "Well, yeah. You want me to find out more?"

"Never mind," I said, and got my ass up outta my chair and walked over to the cell. That ole boy what Butcher had questioned had a right smart mouse up along the left side a' his face. He looked up at me. I was just a-staring at him is all.

"What?" he said.

"This feller what paid you," I said, "what was his name?"

"He never said."

"Where's he a-staying?"

"I don't know."

"What the hell do you know?"

"I was just walking down the alley, and he just kind of appeared right in front of me. I don't know where the hell he come from. He give me this rig to wear and give me ten bucks. I hadn't never saw him before, and I ain't seen him since."

I turned to the other boys, and they give me the same kinda story. Butcher said, "You want me to question them some more, boss?"

"No," I said, "never mind. I expect they're a-telling the truth."

Just then we heared about four or five shots what sounded like they was just right out in the street. Me and Sly and Butcher all hauled out our shooters and headed for the door. I guess Dingle just kept on a-scribbling. Well, the other three of us wound up standing out in the middle a' the street looking all around like three dumb asses. Final we went to walking up and down the street a-looking and asking anybody we seed had they saw anything atall, but they all answered negative. (I learnt that word from ole Dingle. You mighta figgered that out for your own self.) Anyhow, Miller the Churkee come a-running around a corner with his shooter in his hand, and whenever he seed us, he come a-running on up to where we was at, mostly in a cluster in the middle a' the street.

"Where's those shots come from?" he said.

"We're damned if we know," I said. "We was in my office when we heared them. Where the hell have you been?"

"Just checking around town for Cody," he said. "No luck."

"Well," I said, "he's here somewhere. He just sent four bastards into the Hooch House dressed up like his own self, and then come those damned shots."

"I don't know where he could be," Miller said. "I've searched all over."

"Hell," I said, "let's all of us go back to the Hooch House." So we walked over there and took up our usual place at my private table. Aubrey brung drinks all around.

"I don't like this, Barjack," said Sly.

"What the hell?" I said. "Do you think I like it?"

"No, but I like to know who it is I'm dealing with. I like to see him."

"We know who he is, all right," Miller said. "We just can't find him."

We heared four more shots then, and we all of us run back outside. You won't be surprised none to hear that we never seed no one. We give it up again and went back to our drinks. By God, my glass were empty! Some son of a bitch had dranked it all up.

"Goddamn it, Aubrey," I shouted. "How come my glass is empty?"

Aubrey said, "You must've drunk it."

"I never touched it none, not one drop, and then we heared them shots. Who come in here and come over to my table?"

"I never seen no one come in," Aubrey said.

"It was Cody," said Miller. "Who else could it have been?"

Aubrey heared him and said, "I'd have seen that son of a bitch if he'd've come in here."

"He was invisible," said Miller.

"That would explain a lot," said Sly, "but I'm not sure I can believe it."

"I wonder if his goddamn blood will bleed red

or invisible if I was to get a slug into his ass," I said.

Dingle was a-scribbling as hard and fast as ever I seed him scribble. Four more shots come. They sounded like as if they come from way down the street this time.

"He's either the fastest man alive or he has some accomplices," Sly said. Aubrey was a-bringing me a fresh drink. Miller and Butcher jumped up and headed for the door, but I never moved. Whenever Aubrey picked up my empty glass and set down a fresh one, I said, "Aubrey, break that damn glass." I didn't want to be drinking after no ghost nor even no ghostlike feller.

"Yes, sir," Aubrey said, and he just throwed it straight down on the floor and smashed it into a whole bunch a' little pieces.

"Damn," I said. "I never meant to do it right here."

"I'll sweep it up," he said, and he walked back over behint his bar. It wasn't no time before Butcher and Miller come back in with their faces long and their heads a-hanging. They come back and set back down. Aubrey sauntered over with a broom and a dustpan and went to sweeping up the broke glass. Then I heared three shots from the other end a' town.

"Don't bother, boys," I said. "You won't find him."

"He's just tormenting us," Sly said. "Trying to keep us nervous."

"Well, he's succeeding," said Miller.

"I'd sure like to get my hands on that son of a bitch," said Butcher.

Bonnie and Polly come in just then, and they was a-holding ole Happy up betwixt them. They was moving kinder slow on account a' Happy, but soon as they come in the door, Bonnie yelled out at me, "Barjack, what's all that shooting outside?"

"We don't know, sugar tits," I said.

"It's Cody," said Miller. "Keeping us on edge."

The gals made it to the table with Happy, and they put Happy down in his chair, and then they set down in their places. Happy's head was all wrapped up. "Happy," I said, "you hadn't oughta be up yet."

"Aw," he answered, "I'm all right."

Then they was some more shots, but this time they come right in through the front winder a' the Hooch House, shattering glass all over the place. This time we all jumped up with a gun in our hands and headed for the front door. "He's right outside," Butcher yelled. "We'll get him this time," said Bonnie. Me and Bonnie got stuck for a minute trying to get through the door at the same time, but I final broke on through. The only difference between this time and the other times was my broke winder. We all of us wound up standing out in the street looking all around, but we never seed him. Sly, Miller, and Butcher all went on the hunt again, but I headed back for my second abandoned drink. The gals and Dingle and Happy follered me. I was real anxious to see was my drink still there and still untouched. It was, so I set down and tuck me a slug. It were good whiskey, and I hated to think about that slimy bastard a-drinking down a whole tumbler full a' the fine stuff at my expense.

I finished my drink and called for another one,

and then them three what had run off on that wild-goose chase come back and come on over and set down. Sly said, "Barjack, what's your horse doing out front?"

"My horse?" I said. "He's s'posed to be put up in the stable."

"Well, he's right outside," Miller said, "saddled and waiting to go."

"Goddamn it," I said, shoving back my chair and standing up. "I'll get to the bottom a' this shit right now."

I walked outside, and sure enough, my ole horse was just a-standing there, like Miller said, all saddled and just a-waiting for me to come out and climb on. Well, I did just that, and then I rid him down to the stable where he was supposed to be in the first place. I yelled till the stinky stable man come out. Then I got down outta the saddle and handed him the reins. I was about to ask him something, but he beat me to the punch.

"When the hell did you get him?" he ast me. "The last time I looked, he was in his stall."

I went and tole him the whole story and ast him a few questions, but he just stuck to his guns. He hadn't seed no one come in and hadn't seed no horse go out. "Well, keep your goddamn eyes open," I said, and I walked back to the Hooch House. Ever'one there wanted to hear what I had found out, and I said, "Not a damn thing."

Butcher had follered me as far as the front door, and he was still a-standing there just a-looking out into the street. "Hey," he called out. "Ain't this Happy's horse a-coming?"

Happy stood up and walked to join Butcher at the front door, and I heared him say, "Damn. It is. For sure."

Miller stood up just then and headed to join them. "What the hell is going on?" he said. Sly and Polly follered along. Final Bonnie couldn't stand it no longer, and she went over there to take a look for her own self. At last it was just only me and Dingle a-setting at the table, and Dingle was complete wrapped up in his scribbling, so against my better judgment, I got up and joined them. Happy's ole nag, all saddled up, was just a-walking down the middle a' the street.

"Where's he s'posed to be?" I ast Happy.

"Down at the stable," he said.

"Somebody catch him up and take him back down there, and then remind that worthless old son of a bitch what runs the place that I tole him to keep his damn eyes open," I said, and as I turned to head back to my table, I seed Miller head out for the horse. I didn't say nothing for a while, not till Miller got back and set down, and not till he had spoke first. What he said was, "There were a few drops of blood on the saddle."

I said, "I want to tell you all something right up front and right now. Whenever I see that son of a bitch Cody, I mean to kill him. There ain't gonna be no arrest, no jail time, no trial. I mean to kill him. And if any a' the rest a' you takes him alive and puts him into my jail, whenever I see him in there, I'll kill him then."

We was a-dealing with the strangest, most slipperiest, most damned aggravating bastard I had ever come across in my whole entire life, and I didn't mean to take no chances with him no more than what I had to. And I wanted that plumb understood.

"Say," said Happy, "whose blood could that be anyhow? I weren't even in the saddle whenever I got hurt."

"What could it mean?" said Polly.

"I think it's a prediction," Miller said. "It means that there's coming a time when our horses will all have empty saddles."

"We'll all be dead," said Sly. "It's more psychology."

"Sike whut?" I said.

"What he means, Barjack," said Dingle, looking up from his scribbling for the first time, "is that Cody is working on our minds."

"Hell," I said, "I knowed that." And I did too. Sort of. I seed a article on the subject in a damned newspaper over to the county seat one time. And I read it too. Well, most of it.

"It was likely chicken blood," said Miller.

"What was?" Butcher ast.

"The blood on Happy's saddle," said Miller.

"Oh. Yeah."

An old boy what was setting close to the front door got up and come a-walking back to my table. "Barjack?" he said.

"What is it?" I said.

"The Widder Tanner is outside the door."

"Yeah?"

"She said she wants to see you."

"Well, let her come on," I said. "I'm just a-setting here."

"She said she ain't never been inside a saloon."

Bonnie elbowed me real sharp. "Go on out and see what she wants," she said.

"Ow," I said. "All right. You don't need to kill me."

I shoved back my chair and got up. Then I picked up my tumbler and drained it dry and walked out the front door to see what the widder wanted with me.

"Barjack," she said, "someboy has stoled three of my chickens."

"How do you know that? Has you counted them?"

"Course I did. I always count them when I feed them. I'm three short."

"They coulda wandered off. Has you got them fenced in real good?"

"Barjack, I been keeping chickens all a' my life. I ought to know when my chickens has got stoled. Well, what are you going to do about it?"

"I'll look into it, Miz Tanner," I said, "and if I catch the damned rustler, I'll see that he gets hunged up by his neck for robbing a poor widder woman."

"All right," she said.

I headed back for my table, and along the way, a thought come into my head. I set back down, and I said, "Folks, that damned Cody, he has for a fact become a chicken rustler, and that blood on Happy's saddle were for sure chicken blood."

"Have you got some news, Barjack?" Sly ast me.

I tole them then about the widder's chickens, and a' course they had all heared what ole Churkee had said about the blood on the saddle.

"So you think that Miller was right about the

blood," said Sly, "and that Cody got it from steal-ing Miz Tanner's chickens?"

"I do," I said, feeling like one a' them new-fangled detectives, "and I'm a-going over to the widder's place right now to investigate the scene a' the crime."

Chapter Twenty-two

Over at the Widder's place we met Miz Tanner in front a' her house, and she went and led the way around the house to her chicken yard, where a dozen or so a' the nasty birds was a-clucking around.

The widder tole us that she had just counted them again right before we come, and they was twelve a' the rascals. I figgered that was already more chickens than anyone in they right mind should ought to want, but the widder went and said that she'd had fifteen a' the shitty birds just a couple a' weeks ago.

I ast her did she hear anything, but she said that they make so damn much noise all the time that if she did, she never noticed. I ast her did she ever see anything, and she said no. We went to leave the chicken yard, and I lurked around till I was the last one in there. I looked around at them damn birds, and I said, "Why don't you damn dumb-ass birds learn yourselfs how to fly? Hell, I learnt, and I ain't even got no wings."

We never found no evidence a' no kind around the widder's place. No footprints nor nothing that would help us. Dingle were a-scribbling like crazy, though, and I sidled up to him and I ast him, "Dingle, what is you writing down there? Is you writing down ever'thing what we finds out here?"

"Yes, sir, Barjack," he said, "I sure for certain am doing just exactly that."

"Well," I said out loud so's ever'one could hear me, "I done ast all a' the questions what I had in my mind, and I done looked around at ever'thing I wanted to look at, so I'm a-heading back for the Hooch House, but if any a' the rest a' you wants to stick around here and look some more or ast the widder some more questions, feel free. She won't mind one little bit."

So without saying nothing else, I turned to leave. Sly fell kinda in step with me, but the rest a' the gang stayed at the widder's place. "Did you see anything, Barjack?" Sly said.

"Hell, Sly, I couldn't even tell if anyone had actual stold a chicken."

"Well, I believe Mrs. Tanner," Sly said. "Someone has stolen three of her fine chickens, and I believe that someone to be Mr. Cody who is trying to torment you to death."

We had just stepped into the street headed back toward the Hooch House whenever a saddled horse come running toward us. Then a couple more. That made all the horses what me and my official posse and my unofficial one had been a-riding. Me and Sly stopped this little bunch, and right off we seed that there was drops a' blood on each saddle. Being down at the widder's place, we was also close to ole doc's office, and so I said, "Sly, let's just lead these here animals over yonder by the doc's." He never said nothing, but he follered along. I went inside and come back out in a minute with ole Doc.

"Looky here," I said, pointing at the blood on one saddle, "and here, and here," I said, pointing at two more. Doc looked and murmured, "Hum, hum."

"Doc," I said, "I wants you to check that there blood and tell me just what is it."

"I can't guarantee nothing, Barjack," Doc said. "I ain't got all the best lab equipment for that kinda work."

"Well, you're all we got, Doc," I said, "so just do your best."

Me and Sly was headed back to the Hooch House whenever Sly just stopped and stood still in the street. He was rubbing his chin and just staring down at the street. "Barjack," he said, "let's go back down to the stable for another look."

I never ast him what for, I just turned around and walked beside of him back to the stable. Whenever we got there, ole stinky seed us and he just got his ass outta the way, and Sly, he went right straight to a ladder leading up to the loft. He clumb up there and disappeared, and I stood down below a-wondering whether I was curious enough about Sly's doings to climb that there ladder after him. So as to keep myself from looking idle or stupid or something like that, I went to kinder poking my head into various a' the stalls up and down the side wall. The old man come out and showed hisself, and I called out to him.

"What do you want with me, Barjack?" he ast me.

"Listen here, Stinker," I said, "three more horses has been saddled and turned a-loose from in here just today, not ten minutes ago. What do you know about it?"

"Not a damn thing," he said. "I been working, not a-watching."

"Someone could come along here and steal my horse right the hell outta your stable," I said. "Or anyone else's damn horse."

"I allus said that if a man is dead set on stealing something, he'll get it," the nasty old fart said. I was just about ready to kick his skinny little ass, whenever Sly distracted my attention.

"Barjack," he yelled out. "Come up here and take a look."

I went to the ladder and clumb on up there. It were kindly dark, so I just stood there squinnying my eyeballs. "Over here," said Sly, and I looked to my left, which was toward the front a' the building. I kinda saw him up there. It was like he was down on his knees or something, but he was just only a black outline, a, you know, a silly wet or whatever they calls them. Anyhow, I started in to making my way slow to him. "What you got?" I said.

As I come close to him, Sly struck a match and helt it up, and then I seed just what he had come across. They was chicken bones and chicken feet and heads and feathers. They was a pool a' chicken blood. They was a spare couple a' long-tailed black coats laying there. There was even a tin platter what had been used to hole a fire in it. And then they was bits a' the crust from around a slice a' bread where it had been et right up to the crust and then tossed aside. They was even a coffeepot and a cup. I stood up and walked over to the edge a' the loft. My eyes was used to the darkness by then. And I yelled out to ole Stinky, "Hey, you old fart, run out and find one a' my depitties and tell him to fetch Dingle the Scribbler and bring him along to right here, and make it quick."

We went on back down the ladder and waited around just a little whilst I lit up a smoke. Then here come Happy and Dingle and even Butcher. I tole them what I had found, and then I tole them to go up there and not to disturb nothing but for Dingle to first write it all down the way we found it. Them three went up that ladder and me and ole Sly, we went back to the Hooch House and set down at my table. Aubrey didn't need to be yelled at or waved at or nothing, he brung us each just what the hell we was wanting. I tuck a good long drink a' my good brown whiskey.

"Sly," I said, "just what made you go back to the stable anyhow?"

"Those last three horses he saddled up and ran down the street," he said. "It would be very nearly impossible for anyone to saddle up and then run out on the street as many horses as he did without being caught unless he had a good nearby hiding place."

"Humph. Yeah. I reckon." I downed the rest a' my drink and Aubrey come a-running with more. "Well, maybe we flushed him out some. Whenever he finds out that we has discovered his hidey-hole, he'll have to go somewhere else. Maybe we'll catch him then."

"Maybe so," said Sly.

"So we know who he is and we know where he's been a-hiding," I said. "Now all we need is to just catch up with the slimy shit."

"That's all," Sly said. He was sipping coffee.

"It looked to me like he was a-cooking up there," I said. "Was he a-cooking up there? Do you think he was?"

"I'd say, pretty definitely, he was cooking up there," Sly said.

"Damn," I said. "We're all damn lucky that he never caught the damn stable on fire. The whole damn town coulda gone up."

"Yes," said Sly, "we've been lucky about that, but we still haven't caught the culprit."

Happy and Butcher and Dingle come in then, and they all come back to my table, and Aubrey brung them all drinks.

"You boys find anything more interesting up there?" I ast.

"We seen matches and something what was used for a firepot," said Butcher.

"Chicken bones and heads and feet and feathers," said Happy.

"Guts off to one side," said Dingle. "And three black coats."

"Humph," I snorted. "We never seed the guts."

"No, we didn't," said Sly. "There could be something else up there yet that we missed."

"Butcher," I said, "go back down there and make sure that no one gets up into that loft. I don't want nothing up there to get disturbed before I get another chance to detectivate around in the loft."

"Yes, sir," he said. He downed the rest of his drink and hurried out.

"Barjack?" said Happy.

"Whut?" I said.

"Do you want me to go and help Butcher?"

"Happy," I said, "if I had wanted you to go and help him, I would have told you to do it."

"Yes, sir."

"Happy, has you ever knowed me to hesitate to let you know when I wanted you to do something for me?"

"No, sir."

"Happy?"

"Yes, sir?"

"Wait about two hours and then go down yonder and relieve ole Butcher."

"Yes, sir," he said. "I'll do 'er."

Miller come in and come on over and set.

"Churkee," I said, "we found out where the invisible man has been hiding out and taking his meals."

"You did? Where?"

I tole him all about the stable and what we had seed up in the loft.

"That's interesting," he said, "but does that get us any closer to Cody?"

"It might force him out in the open some," I said. "It might could help."

The old sawbones come in then, and he looked the place over till he spied us, and then he come a-walking toward us. Whenever he come over close to my table, he said, "Barjack, it's chicken blood."

"All of it?" I ast.

"All of it," he said.

Whenever he left, Miller wanted to know what we had been talking about, and I tole him about the latest horses with blood on their saddles.

"So he was just trying to scare us," said Miller. "Chicken blood on the saddles."

We fooled around like that for about another couple a' hours, and ole Happy, he allowed as how he had ought to get his ass down to the stable to relieve ole Butcher, and then he left, but he were back right quick. He come a-running in. He had done run by Doc's, on account a' he went in the stable and found Butcher laid out on the floor. Well, all of us follered him back to the stable. We found Doc there with Butcher, kneeling over him there where he was stretched out on the floor.

"How is he, Doc?" I blurted out.

"Hell, Barjack," he said, "I just got here."

"Give him time," someone said.

I paced the floor puffing on my cee-gar.

"He's just been banged on the head," the doc said. "He'll be all right."

"He's got a damn hard head all right," I said.

Butcher moaned, and he tried to sit up.

"What happened, Butcher?" I said.

"I was going up the ladder," he said. "You tole me to watch the loft. Right? So I went up the ladder, but I just only got my head above the loft whenever something hit me. That's all I know till just about now."

"So Cody returned," said Sly.

"And ambushed poor ole Butcher," I said.

"You s'pose he could be still up there?" Happy said.

"Why would he want to hang around up there," I said, "after he's been discovered?"

But I was thinking Happy had been right twice just lately and I had been wrong. "I don't know," I said. "He might be."

Happy put his left hand on a rung of the ladder

and slipped out his Colt with his right. Miller stepped up and put a hand on Happy's left. "Let me do it," he said. Happy give me a look. Then he let a-loose a' the ladder and stepped to one side. Miller mounted the ladder quickly, and before I knowed it, he was up on the loft, squatting close to the edge. A bullet exploded, its lead spanging into the board a couple of feet right of Miller's right foot.

He made a dive to his left, and then I lost sight of him. "Son of a bitch," he shouted.

"The same back to you, you dreary little shit," came a voice I tuck to belong to Cody.

"Is that you, Cody?" I yelled out. There was no answer. "You jist as well to give yourself up," I continued. "You're way outnumbered here."

He still didn't say nothing, so I said some more.

"We got you cornered now, boy," I called. "There ain't no way out for you."

Happy nudged me on the shoulder, and when I looked at him, he nodded toward the far end of the room. There was another ladder up to the loft at that end. I looked at it and back at Happy. I nodded, and he headed for the second ladder. He started climbing.

"Cody, you silly shit," I called out, "give it up. You're just going to get yourself all shot up to pieces is all you're a-doing."

"Oh yeah? No one in your army has hit me yet."

Happy climbed up on top and crouched low. And I had heared the voice of the bastard what we all wanted to get. He was up there all right, and so was two a' my depitties. They couldn't see much good up there, though. I knowed that on account a' I had been up there a-looking. It were dark as hell, and they was bales a' hay stacked all around. I weren't none too sure a' Miller up there, on account a' for an Injun, he didn't seem to me to have no patience. Happy would be all right, though, I figgered. Then I heared some fast footsteps, and then I seed Miller stand up and snap off a shot, and I heared a yelp too.

"Did you get the son of a bitch?" I called out.

"He's going out the front," Miller yelled, and I could see enough a' him that I seed he was a-running for the front a' the building. You see, they was a second-story door up there on the front a' the building for the loading a' hay bales. There weren't no steps to it nor no ladder out front. There was just a pully up there with a rope a-running through it. I reckon ole Cody, he had run for that open doorway, and then he had jumped to the rope, grabbing on to it to let hisself down to the ground. Miller was after him from up on the loft, and I went a-running for the front door down below.

Chapter Twenty-three

When I made it to the front door a-huffing and a-puffing, I didn't see no sign a' Cody. It flashed through my head again that he was some kinda ghost or something. I felt goose bumps pop up all over my whole entire body, and I shivered. Sly and Dingle come up beside a' me. Sly just stood looking around, but Dingle, he said, "Where is he?"

"I know right where the son of a bitch is at, Scribbler," I said. "That's how come me to be a-chasing after him just as hard as ever I can go. Can't you tell?"

"Barjack?" It was Miller.

"Whut?" I answered.

"I think he went up, not down."

"What the hell do you mean by that?" I said.

"I mean I think he's on the roof."

"Surround this damn building," I said, and Dingle and Sly and Butcher went a-running to do it. Then I said, "See can we shoot holes in his damn feet." I fired a shot up into the bottom side a' the roof. Miller and Happy went to doing the same thing. I heard one shot fired from outside, and I figgered that one a' them out there had caught a glimpse a' Cody up on the roof. Then I seed ole Stinky-ass a-peeking out from his little office.

"Stinky," I yelled at him. "Has you got a gun in there?"

"Just a old shotgun," he said, his voice a-trembling.

"Well, get the damn thing and help us ventilate your roof."

He come out with it in a couple a' minutes, and he was a-shoving shells into the barrels. "It's a hell of a note when the law forces a man to spoil his own roof," he said.

"It's the best way I know of for you to get a new roof," I said. "Now get to shooting, goddamn you."

He went and blasted a hell of a hole right up over our heads. I emptied my Merwin and Hulbert and stopped to reload. Stinky shot his second shot up into the roof. I looked up at the gaping holes he had made, and it come to me that he could just blast away the whole roof, and then Cody would fall back through. I could tell that Miller was reloading upstairs. Happy had a couple a' shots yet. I finished up and went to shooting again.

Then here come Bonnie and Polly a-running like hell was on fire. Bonnie's monster tits was just a-bouncing all over the place. Both of them had their guns out, and when they got inside the stable, Bonnie said, "What the hell are you doing?"

"Cody's up yonder on the roof," I said, "and we're trying to put holes in his feet."

They didn't need no more explanation nor encouragement. Both of them went to shooting.

Butcher come up to me and tole me a little plan he had. "Are you up to that?" I said.

"Sure, Barjack," he said. "He never hurt me that much."

"All right then," I said. "Go on ahead."

"Don't nobody shoot me by mistake," he said. Then he run to the nearest ladder and dumb up to the loft. He pulled the ladder up behint hisself, and he carried it over to just under where Stinky had blasted a hellacious hole in the roof. He poked that there ladder up through the hole, and then he started up. He went real slow and cautiouslike. It seemed to me like as if it tuck him a hunnert years to get his head poked up through that hole, but final he did it. He got his head and his gun hand poked through. The rest of us had quit shooting, and I was just a-biting on my lip waiting for a gunshot and hoping it would be Butcher's. But it never come.

Butcher backed down the ladder a step, getting his head back on the inside, and he looked down at me. "There ain't no one up here," he said.

"That ain't possible, goddamn it!" I shouted.

Butcher crawled all the way through the hole then, and he went to walking around all over the roof. He waved down to Dingle and Sly, and by and by, he come back inside through the hole again, and he put the ladder back where it come from and come back down it. He walked over to stand right beside a me.

"No one," he said.

"Happy," I said. "Miller, you just as well come on back down from there."

Well, we was all gathered up together in one bunch again, and I was just about ready to suggest we go back to the Hooch House whenever we heared a hellish scream coming from in the back a the stable. I looked over my shoulder just in the nick a' time to see a big black horse a-slobbering and sling snot all firey eyed and a-running right straight toward us. They was a man in a long-tailed black coat a-setting in the saddle. I don't know who the hell was a-guiding the horse on account a' the man had gun in each hand and he was a-blasting with both. I made a belly dive for the side a' the stable and just in time too. Ever'one else did the same thing.

Whenever he was gone out the door, we all scrambled back up onto our feet, hauled out our shooters, and ran out the front door after him. But we stopped. We looked around. We never seed him no more.

"Goddamn it," I said.

Then from around the corner, here it come again, that black vision from the depths a' hell, and once again, it were a-coming straight at us. We scattered again. I was on the ground again. This time when he went in, he shut the big main door and throwed the latch in place. We all jumped up and tried it, but we couldn't budge it.

"We could get in through the roof if we had a long ladder," Butcher said.

"I'll get one," said Happy, and he run off. He was back pretty quick with a long ladder, and he stood it up against the side a' the stable. He went to climbing up, and pretty soon he had disappeared. About then, Cody stepped up in the middle a' the open doorway to the loft, and he had a lit lantern in each hand.

"Goddamn all of you," he shouted, and he tossed one a' them lanterns down so that it hit the ground and the front wall a' the stable both, and it started flames a-licking up the side a' the building.

"You damned fool," I yelled at him. "You'll burn your own ass up."

"The flames of hell don't frighten me," he shouted, and he busted the other lantern right at his own feet, and whilst the fire started burning up his legs, he laughed. It were a loud and crazy-sounding laugh. Polly tuck aim and shot a bullet right smack into his what you call a sternum. He stopped laughing whenever he jerked from the impact a' the shot, and he stood up there a-swaying in the flames.

Happy opened the front door from inside and started all the horses a-running through it to the outside. Whenever they broke loose they headed all over town.

"Oh, Lordy," ole Stinky said. Happy come out to join us, and he looked up and seed Cody on fire and a-laughing up there.

"By God, Barjack," he said. "What?"

"It's an unholy conflagration," said Dingle. "The fires of hell have come up here to reclaim their own."

"Let's send him on his way a little faster," I said, and we each one of us raised our shooters and fired a shot apiece into the burning madman. At last he fell. I reckoned he was dead. We stood there awhile just a-watching the fire, and then we all walked real calm back to the Hooch House. When we was all setting down and we had our drinks, even Sly, nobody said nothing.

"I think he was a ghost," said Butcher.

"I hope you're wrong," said Happy. "You can't kill a ghost."

The next day some of us sifted through the ashes till we come onto Cody's bones and his guns and his belt buckle. He was gone all right, and we was all glad of it. I had to sign some papers and leave them with ole Peester to okay the town a-paying for a new stable for ole Stinky. Ever'thing was quiet again, and I sure as hell was glad of it. I was setting in my office behind my desk and I give ole Happy a look. "He was a for sure ghost, Happy," I said, "but for sure, we figgered out how to kill him."

Happy kinda grinned. "Yessir, Barjack," he said, "we sure as hell did figger that out."

"Each of Randisi's novels is better than
its entertaining predecessor." —*Booklist*

Robert J. Randisi

Author of *Beauty and the Bounty*

When Lancaster rode up to the ranch house all he wanted was a little water. What he found instead was trouble.
Three men were beating and kicking a woman, and Lancaster couldn't let that be. As the gunsmoke cleared, the
three men were dead. Inside the house was another dead
man, the woman's husband. But who killed *him*? The
sheriff says Lancaster shot them all in cold blood. It's just
too bad for Lancaster that the dead husband was a town
deputy, that the three other men were his brothers, and
that all four were the sons of the local judge—the judge at
Lancaster's upcoming trial!

GALLOWS

"Randisi always turns out a traditional Western
with plenty of gunplay and interesting characters."
—*Roundup*

ISBN 13: 978-0-8439-6178-2

The Classic Film Collection

The Searchers by Alan LeMay

Hailed as one of the greatest American films, *The Searchers,* directed by John Ford and starring John Wayne, has had a direct influence on the works of Martin Scorsese, Steven Spielberg, and many others. Its gorgeous cinematic scope and deeply nuanced characters have proven timeless. And now available for the first time in decades is the powerful novel that inspired this iconic movie.

Destry Rides Again by Max Brand

Made in 1939, the Golden Year of Hollywood, *Destry Rides Again* helped launch Jimmy Stewart's career and made Marlene Dietrich an American icon. Now available for the first time in decades is the novel that inspired this much-loved movie.

The Man from Laramie by T. T. Flynn

In its original publication, *The Man from Laramie* had more than half a million copies in print. Shortly thereafter, it became one of the most recognized of the Anthony Mann/Jimmy Stewart collaborations, known for darker films with morally complex characters. Now the novel upon which this classic movie was based is once again available—for the first time in more than fifty years.

The Unforgiven by Alan LeMay

In this epic American novel, which served as the basis for the classic film directed by John Huston and starring Burt Lancaster and Audrey Hepburn, a family is torn apart when an old enemy starts a vicious rumor that sets the range aflame. Don't miss the powerful novel that inspired the film the *Motion Picture Herald* calls "an absorbing and compelling drama of epic proportions."

To order a book or to request a catalog call:
1–800–481–9191
Books are also available at your local bookstore, or you can check out our Web site **www.dorchesterpub.com**.

Cotton Smith

"Cotton Smith turns in a terrific story every time."
—*Roundup Magazine*

Tanneman Rose was a Texas Ranger turned bad. When he and his gang robbed a bank, he brought shame to the badge. A jury found him guilty, a judge sentenced him, but Rose swore he wouldn't die in prison. Instead he died while trying to escape. Time Carlow helped to capture his fellow Ranger that day at the bank, and now he's investigating a very odd series of murders. Each victim was involved in sending Tanneman Rose to jail. Could it be a coincidence? Or is Rose's gang out for revenge? Or Rose, himself? Time doesn't believe in ghosts—or coincidences. He's got to find the answers and stop the murders...before he becomes the latest victim.

DEATH MASK

ISBN 13: 978-0-8439-6200-0

KENT CONWELL

"A great read. Be prepared for adventure."
—*Roundup* on *Chimney of Gold*

As the moon rises, the night riders come out, sweeping over ranches in the valley, bringing fear and intimidation. Someone wants the owners to sell—badly—but like a few other holdouts, Ben Elliott has sworn not to give up his land for any price. So the night riders have upped the stakes. Once they were content to rustle cattle, but now they've moved up to killing livestock…and murdering men. There's only so much a decent man can take. Ben Elliott has reached that point. It's time for him to fight back. It's time for the nights of terror to become…

Days of Vengeance

ISBN 13: 978-0-8439-6226-0

Paul Bagdon

Spur Award-Nominated Author of
Deserter and *Bronc Man*

Pound Taylor had been wandering the desert for days, his saddlebags stuffed with stolen money from an army paymaster's wagon, when he came upon Gila Bend. It was a wide-open town without law of any kind, haven to gunslingers, drifters and gamblers. Pound might just be the answer to a desperate circuit judge's prayers. He'll grant Pound a complete pardon on two conditions. All Pound has to do is become the lawman in Gila Bend. . . and stay alive for a year.

OUTLAW LAWMAN

ISBN 13: 978-0-8439-6015-0

❏ **YES!**

Sign me up for the Leisure Western Book Club and send my FREE BOOKS! If I choose to stay in the club, I will pay only $14.00* each month, a savings of $9.96!

NAME: _____

ADDRESS: _____

TELEPHONE: _____

EMAIL: _____

❏ I want to pay by credit card.

❏ **VISA**   ❏ **MasterCard**   ❏ **DISCOVER**

ACCOUNT #: _____

EXPIRATION DATE: _____

SIGNATURE: _____

Mail this page along with $2.00 shipping and handling to:
Leisure Western Book Club
PO Box 6640
Wayne, PA 19087
Or fax (must include credit card information) to:
610-995-9274
You can also sign up online at **www.dorchesterpub.com**.
*Plus $2.00 for shipping. Offer open to residents of the U.S. and Canada only.
Canadian residents please call 1-800-481-9191 for pricing information.
If under 18, a parent or guardian must sign. Terms, prices and conditions subject to change. Subscription subject to acceptance. Dorchester Publishing reserves the right to reject any order or cancel any subscription.